CALICO
BUSH

CALICO BUSH

by **RACHEL FIELD**

with the original wood engravings
by **ALLEN LEWIS**

A YEARLING BOOK

Published by
DELL PUBLISHING CO., INC.
1 Dag Hammarskjold Plaza
New York, N.Y. 10017

ISBN: 0-440-41005-3

Reprinted by arrangement with The Macmillan Company, New York, N.Y.
Printed in the United States of America

Third Dell Printing—December 1976

*To my island neighbors
and especially
Captain Jim Sprague*

CALICO BUSH: *An Appreciation*

Many years after reading *Calico Bush* two memories remained clear: the rugged beauty of its setting and the inner courage of Marguerite Ledoux. Reading it again, I realize that the feeling of place and the appreciation of people are the strengths that carry the story, simple in pattern but complex and beautiful in texture.

Rachel Field was fifteen, three years older than Marguerite, when she first visited Maine and fell under the spell of its "island-scattered coast." The strong sense of place had its roots in her love and intuitive understanding of a region where the somber, icy months of winter are long and spring comes late but so suddenly that "almost overnight it seemed, the earth turned from bleakness to vehement green." Marguerite thought, "I do believe that even the birds sing more and the flowers put on brighter colors because the season is so brief." The certain instinct of the artist prompted Rachel Field to divide the story into seasons rather than chapters.

Although Marguerite had been reared gently in prerevolutionary France and, in the new world, was reduced to bondage in a pioneering family, she never commands pity. Reserved, keeping her old self a bit apart from "Maggie," the Bound-out Girl, she responded to respect and friendship and drew the comfort that she needed from the trust and love of the children in her care. Her quiet self-containment gave dignity to her servitude and makes her unforgettable.

Calico Bush derives its title from the low-growing sheep laurel, with its deep pink blossoms, which Marguerite first saw on the rocky shore "springing out of every crack and crevice." Aunt Hepsa explained, " 'Tain't held so choice as the tall kind that grows in the hills, but I think it's pretty. I've heard it called Calico Bush in these parts, an' there's a ballad they sing of it." Marguerite adapted to her new life as the calico bush did to its rugged terrain, growing hardy, resourceful, and bonny. And the ballad that Aunt Hepsa sang to her joined the French songs in her memory, adding gentle overtones to her hard-working life.

Allen Lewis' wood engravings underline the stark beauty of the setting and the courage of a time when merely to survive required the greatest determination and endurance. More than his few illustrations are unnecessary, so vivid are the pictures that the story calls up in the reader's mind.

Thirty-five years have passed since *Calico Bush* was first published. Since then hundreds of pioneer stories have come and gone, but *Calico Bush* still stands out as a near-perfect re-creation of people and place in a story of courage, understated and beautiful.

Ruth Hill Viguers

April, 1966
Wellesley, Massachusetts

MAYPOLE POINT

Wherever you go in the State of Maine
You'll come across some old French strain—
A scarlet thread in the sober skein
Of later settlers, since first Champlain
Charted those islands of the sea
In the name of France and the Fleur-de-Lis.
Changed, misspelled, and lost perhaps,
You can find some yet if you search the maps,
A scattered handful of six or so
With Mount Desert and Isle au Haut.
Those lilies of France were far too frail
For the bitter winters; the northeast gale;
The sharp-toothed ledges; the icy tides;
The bristling spruce on the mountain sides;
For a land that succors a needly tree
Can be less kind to a fleur-de-lis.
It's years now since they were broken and lost;
Sturdier stock has weathered the frost.
But here and there in some far place
A name persists, or a foreign face;
A lift of shoulder; a turn of head;

Along with an Old World chest or bed;
A Breton Bible; a silver spoon;
And feet more quick to a fiddle tune;
A gift for taking the last, mad chance
Because some great-great came from France.

These are the facts, and precious few,
Of a certain Marguerite Ledoux,
A Bound-out Girl, thirteen or so,
To Dolly Sargent and her man Joe,
And their brood of children born and bred
In the pleasant port of Marblehead.
No one knows what sent them forth,
Picking a course part east, part north,
In an open sloop, as like as not,
Piled with whatever goods they'd got;
And no one knows, or ever will,
How they built that chimney and rough doorsill,
Laid on the roof and stuffed each chink,
And deepened the spring that they might drink.

Settlers make mention of births and dying,
But for the rest, there's no use trying.
It's the same long round, in sun and rain,
Sun-up to sun-down, and over again.
Trees must be felled and chips set flying,
Fires must burn and pans kept frying.
There's wool to be sheared, and spun by hand,
And crops wrung somehow from half-cleared land.
Winters of sleet, and storm by night,
Northern summers too brief and bright,

A fight for bare necessities—
Yes, Marguerite knew all of these.
But she is a legend, none the less,
A flowering sprig in the wilderness,
A name blown out of years ago,
A sprightly phantom in calico.

This is her story, and this is why
I think of her when tides run high
On rocky ledges; when some wild bird
Calls with a note she may have heard;
When berries ripen in marshy ground,
Bright as the ones she must have found
In other seasons of sun and rain,
On the island-scattered coast of Maine.

CONTENTS

ILLUSTRATIONS

PART 1  SUMMER

1743 and a fine June morning. Blue water, wind from the southwest, and Marguerite Ledoux taking her last sight of Marblehead as she crouched at the low railing of the *Isabella B.* Farther astern she could see Amos Hunt, master and owner of the *Isabella B.*, at the tiller, with Joel Sargent and his brother, Ira, handling ropes or helping to stow their goods more compactly. Nearer at hand Joel's wife, Dolly Sargent, was seated on an old wooden chest, her eyes also straining against the strong sea sunshine till the last familiar headland should be out of sight. Four small children clustered about her, and a baby filled her broad lap. In her full, brown homespun dress and scoop bonnet, Marguerite thought she looked mightily like one of the hens in their coop up forward. But of this resemblance she said nothing, having learned that Bound-out Girls were not expected to hold opinions of their own, least of all upon the appearance of their masters and mistresses.

"Maggie! Maggie!" She started up, seeing Dolly beckoning to her, remembering of a sudden that this was to be her name now.

"Here's a great hank o' wool to be untangled and wound," Dolly Sargent was saying. "No need to idle the morning away if we *are* bound for dear knows where."

Dolly sighed, and her eyes turned once more to the low line of shore that grew steadily a dimmer, paler blue as the boat carried them on.

Taking the wool from her, the girl moved back to her place amidships. Here she found a small wooden keg between several larger ones and sat down to her task. Her fingers were brown and twiglike, but they moved deftly in and out of the thick blue strands of wool. The sun was higher now, and she pushed the cotton bonnet back on her shoulders, making the strings of it fast against the breeze.

Presently a sandy-headed boy went by with a great leap, tweaking one of her dark braids as he passed, and wrinkling his face up into a wide grimace.

"Ho, Frenchee!" he sang out shrilly, "you'll be black's an Injun 'fore we make port."

The girl did not reply, bending to her work more steadily, though she felt an odd dread as always at the approach of this boy. Caleb Sargent was thirteen, only a few months older than she would be on her next birthday, but he stood a good head and a half above her, and his keen blue eyes and teasing mouth were forever expressing his scorn of all womankind and of Marguerite Ledoux in particular. Sometimes she imagined that he also felt an outsider in the midst of this clamoring group of younger half-sisters and his half-brother. His own mother, Joel Sargent's first wife, had died years before. This morning he was feeling very proud of himself, partly because he had inherited a pair of his Uncle Ira's nankeen breeches, still several sizes too large for him, and partly because he had been given charge of the family livestock—the cow and her calf, the hens and chickens, and four unhappy sheep who kept up a pitiful bleating in the forward part of the ship. With some old planks he had been knocking up a makeshift pen for them. Now he scrambled back to this rough shelter with a twist of rope he had begged of his father.

Captain Hunt watched him go with a dubious headshake.

"Ain't likely to make the headway we'd ought to with such a load forward," he was complaining for the twentieth time since they had put out. "I didn't lot on carrying livestock and all these here young ones when we made our bargain."

"Never you mind that," Joel answered him shortly, "I paid you what you asked in hard silver, every shilling of it, and if you ain't aiming to do your part—"

"Dad blast ye!" the Captain broke in. "I'm not the man to go back on my word once it's given. But I say she sets too low in the water. She ain't trimmed proper."

Words passed between the men. There was more argument as to the shifting of household goods stowed in the cockpit and under cover of the hatches.

It was strange, Marguerite thought, to see the family spinning wheel and churn lashed to the rail along with a chest and settle, and the feather bed and a couple of patchwork quilts spread on wooden benches below in the dark little cabin. Where the light struck through the hatchway, she could make out the bright reds and greens of "The Rose of Sharon" and "The Feathered Star," both familiar patterns and greatly cherished by Dolly Sargent, who had little time nowadays for such fine needlework. Overhead the great canvas sail filled and strained as the *Isabella B.* scudded before the wind. There were patches upon it too—

sharp, white lengths of new canvas set into the older weathered gray. One of these showed jagged and triangular as if a dart of lightning had left its mark there. A sturdily built boat, the *Isabella B.*, larger and heavier than most of the fishing smacks thereabouts, with a blunt-nosed prow that rose dripping with salt spray only to plunge and rise again. An odd-shaped world of wood and rope and canvas in which eleven souls and all their earthly possessions were to live for upwards of five days and nights. Strange indeed, but perhaps no stranger than what had already befallen Marguerite Ledoux in the last twelve months.

She was thinking of this as her fingers moved through the wool, trying to sort out the events that had brought her by varying stages to being there at the beck and call of a family of strangers, on a wooden vessel bound for parts unknown—as unknown to her, at least, she told herself, as these new colonies across the sea had been when she and Grand'mère and Oncle Pierre had set forth all those many months before. It had been just such another blue day, and the port of Le Havre had been brave to see in the morning light. Grand'mère had cried, seeing the last of France, but Oncle Pierre had been in good spirits. He had laughed and planned many things—the house they should have together someday in a part called after King Louis, where it was warm and sunny, with rich lands, where people talked their language and one would fancy oneself in a Little France. There they would pay well to hear him play his violin, and it would certainly not be long before he taught those rich planters' sons and daughters the latest dancing steps. Yes, Oncle Pierre would be a personage there, perhaps the only French dancing master in the New World. The thought had made him hold his head very high and point his toes out even when their ship pitched and the deck grew wet and slanting.

Even Grand'mère had grown resigned and happy, thinking of Oncle Pierre a great man over in Little France, thinking of the new home they would make for Marguerite, whose own dead parents had left her in their hands. It had been a long, long voyage, with sun and storm and fog and variable winds, but they had not minded. Even with food grown scanty and water-soaked they had not minded very much. There were always the plans to talk about among themselves, or if the nights were fine and the sky alive with stars large and small, there had been Oncle Pierre's violin to make music. Such beautiful music as he would play, and so many old songs he knew, both the words and tunes. Sitting there now in the shadow of the *Isabella B.*'s patched sail, Marguerite could sing those same little notes and repeat the same words he had taught her; and yet, for all that, Oncle Pierre was dead and gone. He would never point his toes in their narrow shoes again, nor draw his bow smoothly across the taut strings.

It had happened with the swiftness of lightning. One of the sailors had fallen ill almost within sight of land. Great red sores had appeared on his face, and fever burned in his eyes. It had been a terrible time. One had scarcely dared to look at another's face for fear of seeing the first dread sign. And then Oncle Pierre—Marguerite could not even now let herself think of the day when he had fallen ill. They would not allow her and Grand'mère to go near him. Two old sailors with scarred faces did what they could. But it had been no use at all. She and Grand'mère knelt together on the deck when they buried him at sea;

they told over their rosaries and whispered what prayers they could. After that, the Captain put them ashore at the nearest port. It was not the one intended, but the Captain would take no more risks. He must be rid of his ailing crew and clean his vessel. All Oncle Pierre's belongings had been flung into the sea with him, even the precious violin and bow, so she and Grand'mère had nothing but their clothes and the little money bag with its few remaining coins.

There had been none to welcome them to the port of Marblehead, and Grand'mère was too spent to journey to that far place, named for King Louis, where she would have heard her own tongue. So it was one lodging after another while their money lasted, and then a place called "Poor Farm," which they shared with others even less fortunate. But Grand'mère had ceased to care much by that time. She was too weak to get up from her bed, and often she imagined for days on end that she was in France again. At such times she smiled and sang snatches of the songs Oncle Pierre had sung, and if she forgot the words, Marguerite would join in as she sat beside her with sewing. For Marguerite could sew very well for a girl of twelve. All the women at the Poor Farm had praised her little stitches, and she had showed them how to do fancy scallops and garlands as the Sisters in the convent at Le Havre had taught her. In return they helped her care for Grand'mère and gave her instruction in their language. It had not been hard to learn, although people still smiled to hear the way she said certain words. There was Caleb, for instance, who never tired of mocking her queer r's and the way she could never say her h's.

Remembering Caleb, she looked quickly forward, relieved to see his shock of orange-colored hair bent over the coops. All the rest being busy also, she took this moment to draw from under the front of her dress of coarse gray holland a piece of cord from which hung two small objects. One of these was a plain gold ring, the same that Grand'mère had always worn, the other a button of gilt from Oncle Pierre's best blue coat. She had found it afterwards between two boards of the deck where it had rolled. Such little things, she thought, to have outlasted Grand'mère and Oncle Pierre. Now they were all that remained to her of her past, and as such they were very precious.

People had been kind to her when Grand'mère died, but afterwards they had explained that life would be very different. It was not enough, it appeared, for one to know songs and dancing steps and how to sew and embroider. This was a new, rough country with very different sort of work to be done, and an able-bodied girl of twelve must earn her "board and keep." She remembered what a frightening sound those same words had had. And then they had explained to her that she was to be a "Bound-out Girl." Already those in authority were searching about for a family who would take her to work for them. But the fact that she was French had stood in her way. Several women had come to look her over, only to dismiss her with headshakes when they discovered her birth.

"We want no flighty foreign critters under our roof," she had heard one woman say.

The other had expressed like disapproval and had even hinted that with King George at war with the French across the water, she wouldn't feel she was doing her duty to consort with the enemy. But Joel Sargent and Dolly had not been so particular.

"Another pair of hands and feet are what we're in need of," they had explained, "and so long's she ain't the contrary kind we'll overlook where she was born and raised."

Marguerite had sat by while the papers were being drawn up and signed. She had not understood many of the strange words and phrases, but she had not missed their meaning. From that day till her eighteenth birthday she was theirs to command. She would be answerable to these people for her every act and word, bound to serve them for six long years in return for shelter, food, and such garments as should be deemed necessary.

Hastily she slipped the cord and its treasures out of sight again and, tucking her bare feet under her, went at the wool more vigorously.

This had been in March. Now it was June. Marblehead was well behind them. Save to herself she was no longer Marguerite Ledoux but the Sargents' Bound-out Girl in gray holland and cotton sunbonnet, who answered to the name of Maggie when called.

Her mistress was calling to her now. "Here, Maggie, mind the young ones while I fetch the men some victuals. Their stomachs must be clean empty, their tongues are that quarrelsome."

Marguerite rose quickly to take the baby, and the children flocked about her in turn, their sturdy fairness in marked contrast to her own dark coloring and wiry build. Becky and Susan, the six-year-old twins, were alike as two peas in a pod, a stocky pair with stiff little braids of yellow hair and blue eyes. They too wore sunbonnets and dresses of gray holland, short in the sleeve and neck but gathered round the waist into full skirts that flapped about their bare ankles. Patty came next in order, being four, with Jacob, three, ever close at her heels. Their hair, white and curly as lambs' wool, was sheared close to their round heads, and save for Jacob's short breeches and dimpled chin they too might have passed for twins. The baby, Deborah, called Debby by them all, was eight months old and already showed tufts of light hair under her tight little cap. Her eyes were also very blue and her cheeks apple-round and rosy.

"Keep her out the sun, much as you can," the baby's mother cautioned from the cabin. "It's hot enough to raise blisters on her, and this is no place for her to run a fever, dear knows."

"Yes'm," Marguerite answered as she had been taught, crooking her arm to shade the baby's face.

"This old floor's so hot it burns my feet, it does," complained Becky, standing first on one foot and then on the other.

"You should spread your dress out," Marguerite told her; "and then if you fold your feet under you when you sit, you will not feel it."

She showed them how to do so, and they crouched beside her, all but Jacob, who climbed to the larger keg and sat with his feet stuck straight before him staring out to sea.

"Prenez garde!" Marguerite cried as the boat swung about and the child all but slid off. Then, seeing the blank looks on the small faces before her, she caught herself up quickly: "Take care to hold fast!"

"Yes," echoed Susan, "and take care the boom do not sweep you over the side when they shift it."

They were used to boats, as were most seaport children of that day, and although Jacob was only three he was expected to look out for himself. He did not, however, remain long on his perch, for Caleb, happening by, picked him off by the back of his shirt and set him down with his sisters.

"I'll send you to join the fishes if you don't watch out," he chided before he hurried over to the men about the tiller.

They were discussing charts and courses as they ate thick pieces of bread and cheese out of Dolly Sargent's basket, washing it down with draughts of beer from a keg the Captain had brought aboard.

"There ain't no two ways about it." The Captain spoke up at last. "We'll stick to the inner course if it takes us a week from here to the Penobscot. When I said we'd go outside the shoals I didn't lot on havin' her so down by the head."

"Then we'd best put in at Falmouth," Joel said, pointing with his big leathery forefinger to a place on the chart spread between them. "We'll be 'most out of water and feed for the critters by then."

"Yes," agreed Ira, "it'll give us all a chance to stretch our legs a bit, and Dolly won't look so glum if she knows she'll have another sight of folks and fashions." He smiled his long, slow smile, cutting off a hunk of tobacco from a plug he carried.

"I guess it'll be my last sight of them, and no mistake," she answered him with a sigh. " 'Twas hard enough takin' leave of Marblehead, but I declare I'd feel 'most content to settle down in any huddle of houses now."

"That's the woman of it," her husband retorted. "Neighbors and gossiping from morning till night—that's all you think about. But when it gets so settled a body can see houses on three sides from his own door then I say it's time to be off where there's land to spare."

"Plenty of elbow room, that's what a man needs," put in Ira. "I was commencin' to feel cooped up in Marblehead long afore that man happened along to sell you his eastern land."

"Lots of folks never know when they're well off," Dolly remarked sagely between bites of bread.

"And lots would live and die on a measly acre or two when they might help themselves to a couple o' hundred." There was a light in Joel's eyes that showed he had already taken possession of those new lands. His great hands were crooked a little as if they itched to hold an ax. "Marblehead was gettin' so full of folks you couldn't rightly stir about in it. Sometimes the harbor was so cluttered 'twas as much as you could do to edge a dory in; and the highway the same, with such a lot o' coaches and rigs 'twas a caution to cross it.

"Well, you won't be troubled in no such ways where you're a-goin'." Old Captain Hunt wagged his head knowingly. "If folks depended on coaches to go places there, they wouldn't get very far—no, by Godfrey, they wouldn't!"

"I'm not so sot on farmin' as Joel here," Ira went on, "but I figure if you're by the sea you can always make out."

"You're right about that," the Captain agreed. "You'll never want if you're near salt water. It does you for food and takes you places without waitin' for no road."

His last words jogged Marguerite into sudden interest. She had been listening to the talk idly, her eyes on the endlessly parting waves that the *Isabella B.* plowed through. Now she knew in a twinkling what the Captain had meant. The sea was a road, too—a great, watery highway going all round the world. You had only to put out upon it, and it would take you wherever you wanted to go. She smiled to herself, thinking of it so, likening the hollows between the waves to ruts, and themselves moving over it in a coach without wheels.

Now Dolly Sargent was dividing the remains of the bread between the children, breaking it into as many parts as there were mouths, and smearing each piece with molasses from the sweet-smelling wooden piggin. Caleb was sent to milk the cow for Debby, who had awakened crying.

Soon he was back with a hollowed gourd full, warm from old Brindle. The neck of the gourd had been scooped and perforated to make a nursing bottle, and Dolly Sargent let the milk fall drop by drop into the baby's puckered mouth.

"Take the young ones out from under foot, Maggie," Joel told her. "I can't have 'em raisin' a racket hereabouts."

"And watch out Patty and Jacob don't gaum theirselves all over with molasses," cautioned their mother, "for the Lord knows when I'll get to wash them clean again."

They found a spot in the shadow of the settle and other household goods. Here Marguerite returned to her woolwinding, keeping an eye on the four beside her. Becky and

Susan got out their most cherished possession, a corncob doll clothed in a scrap of bright calico, while Patty busied herself with a handful of shells and Jacob pulled up imaginary fish with a bit of rope dangling over the side.

Toward evening the wind changed. It was necessary to tack and veer continually to make any sort of headway. Captain Hunt kept up his grumbling about their overloading and squinted warily at a low bank of clouds the setting sun turned to a fiery rose.

"Those there clouds are lee-set," he muttered. "They'll mean no good to us."

But for all that the evening was fine and clear. Twilight held long over the water, and with the sun down the air grew cool. After they had all eaten what remained in Dolly's basket and the children had had a drink of milk all round, the three youngest went below to the tiny cabin. Their mother returned from putting them to bed on the hard benches. For a while she sat with Marguerite and the twins, watching darkness come over the water and the first stars appear, very large and sharply pointed. Presently Ira joined them, and even Caleb did not feel it beneath his dignity to draw near.

"There's the new moon," said Becky, pointing to the pale sickle that hung low in the west. "I made a wish on it."

"So did I make a wish on it, myself," Susan said, not wanting to be outdone. "An' they do say if you bow to it nine times you'll get what you wished for." She began bobbing her head so fast her braids jerked up and down stiffly.

"If I had *my* wish," sighed Dolly Sargent, "this here boat would be headin' back the way we come from."

Marguerite heard Caleb sniff at these words, but before he could make any retort, Ira Sargent spoke up in his slow, pleasant voice.

"Ever hear tell 'bout the moon an' the powder horn?" he asked. "An old man told me once, an' he got it from his Granpa back in Scotland."

"Tell us, Uncle Ira, go on." The two little girls pressed closer to him, their eyes bright in the half darkness.

"It was this-a-way," he told them. "Once there was a man out huntin' an' he went a long, long ways, so far he got tired with night comin' on an' all. So he stretched himself out to sleep. But first he reached up an' hung his powder horn up on a little bright yellow hook that he seen hangin' right over his head. Well, he shut up his eyes an' he went to sleep, but come mornin' when he woke his powder horn was gone. Look high he did, an' look low, an' there weren't nary a sign of it."

"What did he do then?" asked the twins together.

"Weren't nothin' he could do, 'cept go on home without it," their uncle went on. "But next evenin' when it got dark he went back to that place where he slept, an' there right over his head was the new moon with his powder horn a-hangin' on it, hooked as nice as could be! So he reached up an' took it back home again."

"Mercy, Ira," chided Dolly Sargent. "You hadn't ought to fill their heads with such foolishness."

Marguerite smiled to herself under cover of the darkness. She felt glad of Ira Sargent and his stories. They made her think of those Grand'mère had told her so often of an evening. She was sorry when he left with Caleb to help light the lanterns from a fire kept burning in an iron kettle.

Dolly Sargent went below, but the twins and she sat on together, their bodies huddled close against the sea chill, their eyes on the star-spattered sky overhead. Many planets and constellations she knew from the nights when Oncle Pierre had taught her to call them by name. These she pointed out to the children, naming them over familiarly as one would mention neighbors.

"See, there is Mademoiselle Vénus. Is she not beautiful tonight? And Monsieur Orion with his belt of little stars, and Les Pléiades over yonder."

Presently their mother called the twins to come below, and Marguerite reluctantly followed. She would far rather have stayed out there as the men were preparing to do than creep between the sleeping children in such narrow, box-like quarters. Even when she had settled herself on one of the hard benches with her head on a bag of meal, she lay awake long after all the young Sargents and their mother were asleep. Through the open hatch she could see a bit

16

of the night sky. A fitful brightness came from the stern
lantern as it swung with the vessel's motion, and now and
again the moving shadows of the men showed as they
handled ropes and shifted sail. She could tell from the
sound of their voices whether they were talking among
themselves or whether the Captain had issued orders. Sometimes she heard Caleb also, his boyish tones shrill against
the deeper ones of the three men.

She slept at last, only to waken to shouted orders and a
great pitching and rolling. The *Isabella B.* was behaving in
a very different manner from her earlier one. Her beams
shivered and shook, her bows plunged and reared, and her
mast seemed about to be snapped off short at any moment.

"Ciel!" she cried, starting up in the darkness, one hand
instinctively reaching for her rosary beads. Remembering
in an instant that she no longer possessed any, she slipped
from between the children, who lay in a warm heap of
arms and legs about her, and made for the hatchway.

How she got up the steps she did not know. Icy-cold
water poured down them, and the whole place was awash.
The *Isabella B.* was careening at such an angle that it was
impossible to keep a footing except by clinging to the rails
and inching along. She could make out the figure of Joel
Sargent crawling in this fashion to join Ira, who was struggling to reef in the canvas. Captain Hunt clung valiantly
to the tiller, though waves swirled up and about him till it
seemed he must be swept away with each fresh deluge.
As he threw his weight against the tiller, he shouted out
orders to the others. But the noise of wind and water was
such that even his deep-sea voice sounded faint and broken.

"Make the stays fast!" Marguerite heard him bellowing,

and then the next moment when he caught sight of her, it was, "Below! Keep below there!"

She would have obeyed had it not been for a sudden shrill cry from the bow. Caleb and the livestock were in trouble. She knew this without the splintering of wood and the terrified lows and bleats to warn her. Hardly realizing what she was doing, Marguerite set herself to go forward. Flattening her body against the side of the cabin she edged along, clinging with one hand to the low wooden rail, and bracing her bare feet against any board that could help her keep a foothold. Whatever headway she gained she must make in the second of lull between waves. They swept over and about her, filling her nose and mouth with salt water. The wind whipped at her wet braids, but she hung on. The men shouted to her; she was past heeding.

Halfway along, a particularly high wave washed over the straining bows, burying them in spray. Seeing it upon them, Marguerite lowered her head, flinging all her strength into the grip of her hands and feet. There came another sharp cry from Caleb, and she looked up in time to see a white mass swept overboard. She did not need the agonized bleating to tell her what it was.

Caleb's makeshift pen had been washed away, but the forward rail still held. Somehow he had managed to lash the cow and her calf to this. By twisting his own body between these ropes he kept himself from going over the side, while with both arms he struggled to hold the three remaining sheep. Earlier in the day their legs had been hobbled, the fore and hind ones being tied together to keep the animals quiet. Now this only increased their helplessness. They were like so many bags of wool at the mercy of every wave. Even as Marguerite crept nearer, there came another lurch and Caleb lost his hold on one. Without knowing how she did it, she freed one hand and clutched at the woolly body.

"Keep a-holt!" she heard Caleb shouting in her ear, and she dug her fingers tighter into the thick wool.

They could barely make each other out in the dark and wet, but the whiteness of the sheep helped to mark the places where they clung. Now and again in any slight lull they shouted a word or so to show that they still hung on. But for the most part neither had any breath to spare.

"Ah, my arm—you will twist it off!" gasped Marguerite as the sheep struggled in a panic of animal terror.

She caught her lips between her teeth lest Caleb should hear her crying with the pain. After a little it did not hurt so much. Either the sheep had tired itself, or she had grown used to the strain. She felt very cold and numb and almost too spent to be afraid when the *Isabella B.* took some especially high sea or plunged from watery height to hollow.

And then it was over. The squall passed almost as suddenly as it had come upon them. The wind no longer tore and tugged at the rigging, and in the early light of morning the sea grew quieter. Ira Sargent was the first to reach them. His face looked pale under his sunburn as he peered over the wreckage to see if they were still there. Without a word he took the sheep from Marguerite's hold, leaving her free to crawl aft. She could scarcely grip the wooden rail with her fingers so cramped, and she was too soaked to care that a foot of water slopped about the cabin floor with every lurch and roll.

"Never lotted on seein' that pair of young ones alive," she heard Captain Hunt saying to Joel as she stumbled down the hatchway.

"Well, I guessed Caleb would stick fast," the other answered, "but why *she* ain't gone to bottom traipsin' out there in all that blow is past me. She's got grit, wherever she was raised—I'll say that for her."

"Yes, she's quite a craft, that girl," the Captain added, and then he was shouting orders to Ira about letting out more sail. Marguerite tumbled in a heap on the hard bench below. The children whimpered on all sides, and Dolly Sargent scolded her for her rashness, but this was nothing to the inner glow she felt as she remembered the words she had just heard. The Captain had praised her, and Joel Sargent had admitted that she had grit. Perhaps even Caleb would be less scornful of her now. She fell asleep and dreamed herself back in Le Havre in the sunny garden of the convent. The Sisters were moving about in their soft blue robes and starched headdresses that were like crisped white wings, and the chapel bell was ringing for noonday mass.

She awoke with a dull ache in her head and a body so stiff it was all she could do to keep from crying out as she painfully climbed from the dark cabin into the brightness above. The sun stood high overhead, and the sea was so smooth and blue it seemed impossible it could ever have buffeted the *Isabella B.* so fiercely. But all about were signs of that struggle. Part of the forward railing was gone. One of the hencoops and more than half the precious household goods had been washed away. Dolly Sargent sat in the midst of the younger children, mourning the loss of her possessions in no uncertain terms, while her husband reminded her that it was a mercy they hadn't all followed them to the bottom.

"You'd best be thankful we saved three o' the sheep," Caleb told her with pride. "But for Maggie an' me there wouldn't be so much as a snag o' wool left."

"An' what good are sheep to me without a spinning wheel?" she answered him shortly, turning one of the quilts the better to dry it in the sun.

But for all her fault-finding, Dolly Sargent was easy with her Bound-out Girl that day. She set her no tasks beyond looking out for the children and even gave her a bit of tallow to rub on a great bruise that had risen on her forehead. Already it was turning a deep purple, a sight which seemed to gratify Caleb.

"My," he said, "but you're easy battered. Guess I'm tough's a bear, or I'd be black an' blue all over."

"Oh, hush up," his uncle Ira told him good-naturedly. "Whatever it was struck her warn't no feather."

There being only enough milk for the baby and the two younger children, besides some hardtack, the men set about finding other food.

"What would you say to a taste of Marblehead turkey?" suggested Captain Hunt. "Wind's light enough to spare two hands from the ropes."

Marguerite looked her amazement at these words, and Ira smiled as he and Caleb brought out hooks and lines. Even the twins were less ignorant of such matters than she. They soon explained to her that it was codfish they were after, not wild fowl. With some hoarded bits of dried fish for bait, they cast their lines over the side, and soon several speckled cod and a haddock or two were flopping under foot.

Meantime Joel Sargent had rekindled a fire in the old iron

kettle, sacrificing a stick or two of wood from the broken hencoop which he had been drying in the sun. It took him a good while to whittle off shavings and to get these alight with his flint and steel, but as last it was blazing well and Dolly's spider heating in readiness. Caleb was an old hand at cleaning fish, and soon they were ready to eat.

"Nothin' tastier 'n a cod fresh out o' water," said the Captain as he finished his and tossed the backbone overboard, "an' if I'd a piece o' hot johnnycake besides, I wouldn't swap with King George himself."

But Dolly Sargent felt otherwise. "Half-raw cod an' no salt to season 'em ain't my idea of a proper meal," she told him.

"Cook 'em in sea water next time an' see if they're more to your fancy, Dolly," laughed Ira.

"We'll boil you down some brine soon's we get ashore," her husband comforted her. "Or maybe there's some o' the sheep's salt I can get at below."

Marguerite could not relish hers, feeling still too spent and weak from the night's storm.

About sunset Captain Hunt steered the *Isabella B.* close to shore—a steep coastline of jagged rock with thick-set evergreen trees growing down to the cliff's edge. Against the clear pale yellow of the sky the trees appeared very wild and tattered, like gaunt hosts in an endless procession.

"Never see so many trees in all my born days," said Becky as the children crowded to the rail.

"You're goin' to see a heap more 'fore long," the Captain told them.

Dolly Sargent said nothing to this, but Marguerite noticed that she drew her cloak closer about her. It was only when they passed by a small clearing with three or four houses in it that she showed any signs of interest.

"Those folks are cookin' supper," she said. "I can tell by the chimney smoke."

It was true. All the chimneys had straight gray threads of smoke rising from them, and in the scallop of a harbor several boats were moored. The sea was quiet as they passed. In the stillness a dog's bark came to them quite clearly.

That night they cast over the *Isabella B*.'s anchor and lay till daylight off a high promontory. Cape Elizabeth, Captain Hunt had called it, cheering them with the assurance that next morning they would reach Falmouth. All their spirits rose at this, especially Dolly Sargent's. She was almost gay as she doled out the hasty pudding she had stirred up from their rather water-soaked cornmeal. Ira joked with her as they ate.

"I expect you'll be a rare treat to those folks in Falmouth, Dolly," he said. "I doubt they've seen a bonnet like yours before."

"Or ever will again likely," she answered, pinching at the stitched cloth of its brim. "That wettin' took out what gimp it had. Still, I'm thankful to have one at all after last night."

Marguerite could hear them as she sat in the dimness of the cabin, rocking Debby to sleep in the little wooden cradle which had miraculously escaped the fate of the other pieces of furniture. Since there was no one by to hear or chide her for using the French words, she sang the refrain of a lullaby she had learned of Grand'mère long ago.

Do, do, l'enfant do,
L'enfant dormira bientôt.
Do, do, l'enfant do,
L'enfant dormira tantôt.

Next morning, with sunrise scarcely faded out of the sky, they were tacking between wooded islands, very green and pleasant with a farm or two set in clearings on the larger ones. The Captain was in familiar waters here, having come several seasons back for fishing, but he was too busy picking his course and giving orders for shifting sail to answer Dolly's questions about names and inhabitants. At last they could make out Falmouth, its houses scattered along a wide harbor of smooth water where a number of fishing smacks and a half-dozen larger vessels rode at anchor.

"Not near so many houses as I thought," remarked Caleb, squinting his eyes to blue slits the better to see.

"Marblehead was lots bigger," said Susan.

"Well, it looks good to me," their mother told them. "I'm fair hankerin' to go ashore."

"They've got a church steeple anyhow," Becky pointed out.

"Yes, and a battery," cried Caleb. "See the cannon on top!"

"That's the fort I've heard tell of," explained Ira as he hurried by on his way to shorten sail. "They need to keep a sharp watch out for French an' Injuns."

"Hear that, Maggie!" crowed Caleb with a grimace. "Maybe they'll fire at you."

"No, no," shrilled Jacob, clinging to Marguerite's skirts in sudden terror. "Not shoot Maggie!"

"There, there," put in Dolly Sargent. "Quit your crying, Jacob. They'll not do any shooting if folks behave theirselves. 'Tis only Injuns and the wicked French in Canada they're after."

Marguerite's cheeks flushed under their sea tan. She reached down and took Jacob's hand in hers. This was not the first time she had heard such words about her people, and it was not to be the last. They left a soreness round her heart which persisted in spite of the warmth of the child's clinging fingers and the quick chatter of the little girls.

"I would they were not at war," she thought. "Why must they fight each other all these miles away in a new land?"

But already the men were casting anchor and making the dory ready to swing over the side. Some little distance from the town they could see a slope of green meadowland going down to a salt inlet. Blue flags grew by the water's edge, and a number of cattle were feeding, their backs tawny in the sun.

"I'll warrant it's good pasturage there," Joel Sargent said. " 'Twould be better to land the stock to graze, but I doubt we could haul 'em aboard again."

"No, we'd a time hoisting 'em from the raft in Marblehead," Ira reminded him. "Put Caleb and the young ones ashore there. He can cut enough grass to last the rest o' the voyage while we make for the port."

This was agreed upon, though the twins complained bitterly that they were not to see Falmouth, and Caleb looked his disgust at being consigned to the company of Marguerite and the children. The dory was stoutly made, fashioned for rough weather. It had once been painted a deep yellow, and there was a mast and a sail which could be hoisted, besides two pairs of heavy oars between wooden pins. These Ira and his brother pulled, while Caleb sat astern and worked another as rudder. Marguerite watched the men bend to their oars from her place in the bows with the children, who cried out in high spirits at each dash of salt spray on their faces. And so the dory grated on a strip of pebble beach, and they came ashore.

"I got plenty o' chores to keep me busy," Caleb said importantly as he swung the sickle he had brought to cut the grass. "So you young ones stay with Maggie and don't come mucklin' me."

Grass felt cool and soft to their feet after the hot boards of the *Isabella B.*, and farther up from the water wild strawberries grew in abundance. Marguerite had never seen them so thick and red, and not even those that the market women at home brought to sell in their shallow baskets had ever tasted so sweet. The children filled their hands and mouths. Little Jacob's and Patty's lips were soon scarlet-smeared, but the twins helped Marguerite to fill a small splint basket she had fetched along. She showed them how to line it first with flat green leaves as Grand'mère had taught her. They made a great to-do about the berries they dropped in, but more went into their own mouths.

"Ah," sighed Marguerite, "but they are sweet. As good to smell as to eat. Already my fingertips are delicious."

"I guess Caleb'll want this whole basketful hisself," remarked Susan, looking towards the lower part of the meadow, where they could see him at work. "He'll be that hungry after cutting the grass."

"Well, he'll not get these, shall he, Maggie?" Becky broke in. "I lot on havin' some for my supper."

"Then you'd best drop in more," cautioned Marguerite. "I doubt you've put in twenty all told."

When the basket was filled they went to rest by a clump of birch and spruce. The twins had brought along Jerusha, their corncob doll, and Marguerite showed them how to fashion a fine green dress for her from two large leaves, with daisy heads stuck in for a pattern.

"I'd admire to have one such myself," declared Becky, "of green cloth with white posies all over."

"Ma says we're lucky to get plain holland or bunting," Susan reminded her, "but maybe when we're old enough to marry we'll have sprigged calico."

"I wore printed dresses in France," Marguerite told them. She seldom spoke of such things with the others about, but here with the children she felt more at ease. "Yes," she went on, her dark eyes shining with remembrance, "in summer there was one with small green vines on yellow stuff, and in winter a brown challis with little roses and marguerites. We chose it because of my name, only you call them daisies instead."

"Ma says she won't call you by no such Frenchified name," Susan pointed out.

"Oh, duck your head, quick!" broke in Becky, as a dragon-fly went over them, its wings a shimmer of blue and silver in the sun.

"But why?" Marguerite asked of them as the children all ducked with little excited cries. "Why do you do that?"

"It's the Devil's Darning Needle," piped up Jacob, burying his round head in her lap. "Oh—oh, mustn't let it get you."

"Now it's gone," Marguerite reassured them. "Come, let's gather more flowers to make ourselves wreaths."

But they had hardly sallied forth into the meadow again before they heard a great barking. Something quick and yellow was moving towards them through the grass. In another moment a half-grown dog with a wagging tail and eager red tongue was in their midst.

"Chien, chien!" cried Marguerite delightedly as he jumped up to lick her hand.

He was all friendliness and affection, running from child to child, but always returning to Marguerite as if her touch pleased him most.

"Wonder who he belongs to?" the twins asked of each other. "Watching the cattle, most likely."

"I wish he was our dog," said Patty, and Jacob nodded solemnly and held firmly to the fur about its neck as if he would never let go.

Suddenly they were aware of someone coming toward them—a tall man in rough clothes with a musket over his shoulder. He moved swiftly, with a strange quietness. It struck Marguerite as curious that he did not hail them till he was very near.

"Whose young ones be you?" he asked shortly, in such a stern voice that the two younger children, clung to Marguerite's skirts, and the twins regarded him with scared blue eyes.

"We are from the vessel—yonder," Marguerite answered politely, pointing to the *Isabella B.* anchored off the point. "We have come here for grass and berries."

"Strangers, eh?" The man looked somewhat less forbidding as he rested his arms on his musket and regarded their little group curiously. "Where do you hail from?"

"We came from Marblehead," Susan told him, having gained her voice once more.

"But we're bound up that-a-way," Becky added, waving her arm to the line of shore beyond the harbor and houses.

"Oh, you be, eh?" the man still regarded them intently. "Where's your folks?"

"They went to the town," the twins told him, "but our brother's down there cuttin' grass."

"Guess I'd best have a word with him," said the man, and under his breath he added. "Might's well know what they're in for now, 'fore there's any scalps lost."

They moved towards the shore in a little procession, the children ahead with the dog at their heels and the stranger last of all, musket on shoulder.

"That your dog?" said Jacob at last, summoning all his courage.

"No," said the man shortly. "Must have followed me."

Caleb saw them coming a long way off and left the grass he was stacking into bundles to join them. He and the man drew apart a little, but Marguerite could hear bits of what they said. Her heart seemed to stand stock-still within her as she listened, and though the sun was in mid-heaven and beating hot on her head and shoulders, she turned cold at the words.

" 'Tain't deemed safe for young ones to be out alone in these parts," the stranger was saying. "I'm here now to guard the cattle. Injuns! Why, these woods are full of 'em. Ain't hardly a week but they're up to their devilments."

"You mean they make raids, and kill folks round here?" Caleb asked, and Marguerite thought his eyes grew uneasy as he put the question.

"That they do. We've the stockade and fort now, so

they dassent attack the town same's they used to, but let anyone go abroad and his scalp's not safe. Four men and a guard plowing in sight of the town were killed last month, and a man named Pomeroy settled farther up this tidewater was shot down at his own door coming in from milking and his wife and children carried into captivity."

Marguerite stood in the sunny grass with the children about her and listened. His words made a queer drumming in her ears, but she went on weaving daisies into the wreath she had begun for Patty.

"Guess your folks ain't heard tell much 'bout Injuns up in Marblehead to leave a parcel of young ones off here without a musket among you."

"I can fire a musket," Caleb spoke up. "Trouble is, I haven't got one yet, but I'd make out—some way."

"That's what the folks thought down Sheepscot way last fall when they went gathering nuts. A whole party of 'em—and not five got back alive! Even the islands ain't much safer 'n the mainland. Three cows and six sheep they killed on Great Chebeague a little while back. For spite they done it, an' left 'em half-burned on the beach. No, boy, there's no tellin' who they'll fire on next, and it ain't only old folks' scalps they've got strung to their belts."

After a while their visitor turned to go back to his lookout place in the fork of a tree higher up, promising to keep his eye on them till the dory should come. The children stood about in a scared little group, and even Caleb seemed strangely subdued by what he had heard. But the yellow dog did not follow.

"He wants to stay along of us," said Becky, but it was Jacob who ran after the man, tugging at his free hand and pointing eagerly.

"You can keep him for all of me," they heard him answer the child. "He's been hanging round the fort these many days."

The children were jubilant. Even Caleb and Marguerite felt less troubled by what they had heard as they watched him running to fetch back the stick Jacob threw.

"Maybe they'll not let us keep him," suggested the practical Susan. "Dogs do eat a lot, Ma says."

"He can have some of my supper every night," declared Jacob, with Patty eagerly adding offers of hers.

Caleb had said nothing, but Marguerite noticed that he gave the dog's head a pat as he went off to finish the grass bundles. This she felt to be an unspoken sign that he was on their side.

"He'd ought to have a name," Becky reminded them.

This was a matter for serious consideration. They were still discussing it when the dory came in sight with Joel Sargent and Ira pulling hard at the oars. The children fairly tumbled over one another to reach it first as the men brought it up on the beach. Soon there was an incoherent babble about dogs, Injuns, and a man with a musket. Marguerite stayed a little apart, the dog at her heels as if he too knew himself to be an outsider. The touch of his muzzle pressed in her hand was good to feel. It was a comfort to hear he was to be accepted.

"Well, bring him along then," their father had answered the children's pleas. "He may come in handy scarin' off Injuns. But if he don't behave, over he goes, mind you."

That night, although they ate heartily of fresh food from Falmouth and the wild strawberries were sweet to taste, there was little talk and cheer aboard the *Isabella B.* Dolly Sargent had greeted her children with a rare show of affection, and Marguerite guessed that what they had heard from the man with the musket was already known to her.

After the younger ones were asleep talk and questioning began. No doubt as to what was uppermost in all their minds now. Marguerite listened with the dog's head resting on her knee, and a chill came on her as she heard.

"Comin' home from church they were"—Ira was repeating some tale—"when the Injuns begun firin' at 'em from behind trees. Only one got back to give the alarm, an' he crawled to the garrison half shot to pieces."

"Pesky lot, Injuns are," Captain Hunt went on. "Ain't had much trouble for 'most ten years; lived real peaceable but for small pilferin's. An' now they've broke out again. It's these here Tarratines that's makin' the mischief. They're worse 'n Penobscots or Passamaquoddies long's the French pay 'em a bounty on every English scalp they can show."

"An' that's where we're a-headin', Joe!" Dolly's voice broke in sharp and anxious. "Right into their own country. You heard what they told us."

"Now don't you go believin' all you hear," her husband tried to soothe her.

"But I saw those thirty Injun scalps with my own eyes," she reminded him. "You saw 'em, too, hangin' on poles by the fort. Ten more they needed, they said, to even up with the white ones taken this last twelvemonth. An' that ain't takin' account of the women an' children carried off to Canada. That's what I'm the most feared of, Joe. I'll not dast to let the children out of my sight."

"Other folks have raised young ones in such places afore this," he answered. "I put all I've got into takin' over that claim an' I mean to hold it, so keep your courage up an' we'll make out."

"I'll be needing a musket of my own, Pa," Caleb spoke up.

With morning the dread lifted somewhat. It was impossible to be so fearful with the water smooth as a polished blue floor and every new headland they skirted a fine green adventure. Always the trees were more straight and pointed, pressing closer to the rocky headlands and deeply indented coves and tidewater inlets. Island followed upon island, bristling with untouched spruce for the most part, though occasionally boasting a farm and a cleared field or two.

"Got more islands 'n folks hereabouts," observed Becky.

"Yes," her mother agreed, "seems if we'd passed a hundred since mornin'."

Some the Captain knew by name from his charts and previous voyages. There was Monhegan, which he showed them that afternoon—a dark, humped shape rising several miles out to sea. There, he said, was the finest fishing anywhere save off the Banks. It was even said that the Norsemen had known it years before other white men sailed along the coast. A small group of fishermen and their families lived there in the shelter of a nearly landlocked harbor. In summer they did quite a trade in dried fish with coasting vessels.

Towards sunset they sighted another large island some miles out. Isle au Haut, the Captain called it, explaining that it had been so named by the French. Once again Marguerite quickened to the sound, though Caleb grew scornful.

"Ain't there enough English ones," he complained, "without their puttin' on Frenchified airs?"

Marguerite sighed. But for once the Captain was on her side.

"I always hold it's bad luck to change a name," he said, "whether 'tis an island's or a vessel's. There was good Frenchmen in these parts, same's bad. Yonder a ways is Castine, named for some Baron or other that settled it years ago. He built him a fort there an' a town they said it was a wonder to see in the wilderness. Took him an Injun wife he did, too, an' carried her back home to France with him when the English drove him out under the Treaty."

"An' a mercy it was they did," remarked Dolly. "Such goin's on! I'd think shame to tell of them if I was you." And she gave Captain Hunt a severe headshake.

"Well, he kept peace with the Injuns at any rate. Warn't no such raids an' scalpin's while he was round."

Marguerite dared not show her pleasure in what she had heard, but long after the talk had changed to other matters she treasured the Captain's words. These savages could not all be so terrible if a Baron of France had taken one for his wife. Of that she felt certain.

That night they anchored in the lee of several small islands. Less than another day, if the wind held, and they would reach their own point; but it was a difficult course to pick, the Captain said.

"My, but it'll seem good to sleep under a roof again," said Dolly. "I only hope that house you took over with the claim is built foursquare an' solid."

"He allowed 'twas of the best pine boards anywheres about, Flint did," her husband assured her, "an' tree-nailed. I made sure of that 'fore I bought him out."

But they slept aboard the *Isabella B.* the next night as well, for fog came down from the east, in a thick gray wall.

"Nothin' for it but to set," Captain Hunt had announced when they woke to find themselves shut in fast. "Even if there was wind enough for me to edge along I wouldn't risk gettin' up on one of these ledges. No, Penobscot Bay's no place for that without you know every island and point in it."

It was tiresome waiting there in the chill grayish light. When they went below, the little cabin was filled to over-flowing, and if they stayed above the damp gathered in drops on their hair and faces. Clothes clung clammily, and the *Isabella B.* dripped from stem to stern. Marguerite sat huddled in the opening of the hatch, her feet tucked under her for warmth and her fingers busy with knitting. She and Dolly Sargent were already turning the wool into stockings and mittens against cold weather. Marguerite was able with her needles. The four bone sticks moved swiftly though the fingers that held them felt stiff with the chill. Jacob and Patty sat below her on the next step, little drops forming on their short fair hair. Caleb was learning to box the compass under Captain Hunt's direction. They could hear him repeating the points over and over in a singsong that seemed almost a part of the water slapping at the vessel's sides and the creaking of boards and anchor ropes. "No' No' East," he was droning. "East No' East; East So' East; So' So' East."

A gull flew overhead with a shrill cry, so low they could see its orange feet flattened against a white body, and the bright, restlessly moving eyes.

"Sea gulls lookin' out for fish," remarked Ira as he came by. "Likely we'd best do the same."

"They are wise birds," Marguerite answered, more at her ease as she always was with him. "They need not say 'No' No' East' to know where they are going."

Ira laughed so that his teeth showed strong and white in his sunburned face.

"Yes," he said, "there's times a bird has it easier 'n folks, for all their learnin'."

The men made another catch of cod and haddock, Dolly Sargent cooking them over a fire in the iron kettle round which the children gathered for comfort. Pumpkin, as the dog had been christened because of his color, hung about, catching such scraps as were tossed him. In those two days he had become one of them. His every move and look belonged to the pattern of this adventure in which each of them there had a part.

"He's got the softest tongue," Becky said as the dog licked her hand.

"Yes," added Susan. "An' that's a queer thing. Uncle Ira, what for have dogs got smooth tongues and cats rough ones?"

"If I knew the answer to that I'd be wiser 'n the Man in the Wilderness," he told her. "Do you recollect that old rhyme they used to say to us back home, Joe?

> The Man in the Wilderness says to me,
> "How many strawberries grow in the sea?"
> I answered him as I thought good—
> "As many red herrings as grow in the wood!"

"Trust you to remember the foolish sayin's an' forget the rest," returned Joel Sargent with a shrug.

But the children repeated the rhyme after Ira till they knew it by heart, and Marguerite stored it away as a treasure in her mind.

By midmorning of the next day the sun burned off the fog and they could continue on, though with the wind still easterly they made slower progress and must keep closer to shore. Still the children were in good spirits again, watching each new island and rocky promontory, and Joel Sargent seemed possessed of a new vigor as they approached their goal.

There was still a hint of fog in the air and a far white bank on the horizon, and then suddenly, as Marguerite stood at the wooden rail, her eyes shaded against the brightness, a miracle of mountains came out of the sea. Like dim, blue monsters swimming away from land they loomed to the northeast directly over the *Isabella B.'s* blunt bow. The rich green and tawny browns of the nearby shores only served to make the apparition more strange and unearthly. Marguerite caught her breath, and her heartbeats quickened to the sight.

"Mount Desert," she heard Captain Hunt explaining. "See, there 'tis on the chart."

"*I-s-l-e   d-e-s   M-o-n-t-s*," Caleb was spelling out, "*D-é-s-e-r-t-s*. Queer kind of a name for such a great island."

"A Frenchman, Champlain, that first sailed up this way charted it so on his maps," the Captain explained, "account of the hills bein' so high from the water and bare on top. Look 'most as blue as indigo they do, today, but if you was to sail up close you'd see they warn't. I've cruised along there. It's a sightly place."

"We'll see 'em from our point," Joel told Dolly with pride. "I recollect he told me that, Flint did. He said we'd find no finer prospect all up an' down the coast."

Marguerite was glad that Caleb was not by to see the tears that stood in her eyes. The mountains had been blue and beautiful enough before, but now that she knew them by name they would be different to her. She felt sure that Grand'mère and Oncle Pierre would feel easier about her if they could know this, that there still remained a French name to bear her company in this strange, thickly wooded country of islands and rocky shores.

But points nearer at hand soon engaged the Sargent family's attention. Ira and Caleb did the Captain's bidding in the matter of shifting sail and shortening or letting out the ropes, while Joel eagerly compared each headland and island they passed with the rough chart where his own claim had been marked. A queer tenseness was on them all. Even the animals seemed to sense this, turning their heads shoreward and sniffing alertly.

"Only a couple more headlands to pass an' we'll see it," Joel said to the little group about him. "It's all same as it's written here. There's Old Horse Ledges to the east of us, an' that little pair they call The Sisters, an' the bigger one beyond is Sunday Island. Folks by the name of Jordan have settled there. I can just make out the clearin' an' house. They'll be our nearest neighbors, I guess."

"Smoke's comin' out of their chimney," Susan pointed out presently.

"Praise be for that," said Dolly Sargent, hugging the baby closer.

Marguerite saw that her cheeks were flushed with excitement and that she had pushed her bonnet back from her forehead the better to see. Jacob and Patty pressed close, their hands reaching for hers.

"Look over that-a-way, Maggie," Patty said, "an' watch for our house."

"Our house that-a-way," Jacob repeated after her, pointing to the thickly wooded point ahead.

"There'll be a cove an' a good landin' beach," Joel was saying, "with one side spruce woods an' the clearin' on the other. Yes, the house looks to be on the far side, set maybe a hundred an' fifty yards up from the water line. You'll see."

No one aboard spoke as the *Isabella B.* nosed her way round that last point. Surf made a soft thundering below dark cliffs, and a sea gull started up crying from a weedy ledge. That was all.

Marguerite's heart was beating hard under the waist of her holland dress. Her fingers tightened about the children's hands as they all three pressed close to the rail. Then, suddenly, she felt a queer numbness. There were the cove and the strip of pebble beach even as he had said, with the woods on one side and the cleared piece on the other; there was even a worn line of path going up from the water to the place where the house should have stood. But the house itself was missing. Empty and solitary, the patch of open green spread before them in the late afternoon light.

No one spoke for a full minute. Joel Sargent stared dully before him, the chart limp between his fingers. Caleb and Ira stood rooted in their places, and Dolly's eyes were almost as wide as the children's.

Jacob was the first to break the silence. "Where is it?" he cried out shrilly. "Where's our house?"

"The Lord knows," his mother answered him, and her voice shook.

Marguerite was never to forget the next few hours or the despair that settled on them all, more chill and heavy than the fog which had closed round their boat the day before. Dolly's broad face was drawn into new lines of trouble; Joel Sargent's looked grim as granite under his sunburn, and even Ira had no word of cheer for the scared children and Marguerite as he landed them in the second boatload. The sun was slipping behind the ranks of crowding spruces, but still they lingered in a woebegone little group about the blackened ruins of a cellar at the head of the path.

"Here's where 'twas," Joel kept repeating, as if that somehow made a difference. "There's part of the chimney, made from stones lugged up from the beach, same's Flint said."

"Don't talk to me of him," Dolly broke out bitterly. "He tricked you into takin' this claim. I mistrusted there was no good in it, else why would he be leaving? But you wouldn't listen to reason, an' now look where you've brought us—not even a roof over our heads!"

"I'll raise another one for you, Dolly," Joel answered her. "You an' the young ones shan't want for one long's there's trees an' axes to fell 'em with."

Before she could answer him there came a hail from the water. Two men in a dory were rowing into the cove. Pumpkin ran barking toward them, and the others hurried after. Marguerite came last with Debby in her arms and the younger children at her skirts. One of the strangers was gray-haired and stooping, the other about Ira's age with a powerful body and a square, dark face. They were speaking to the rest. Marguerite could tell it was something grave and important even before she drew near enough to hear. While she was still some yards away she distinctly caught the word "Injun."

These two were Seth Jordan and his son Ethan from Sunday Island, and the news they brought was in no way cheering. Raids by the Tarratines to the eastward and Canada had been more frequent and disastrous of late. It was for this that Flint and several other families had quit their claims for less dangerous parts. No, they explained, the house had been standing when Flint went, but the Indians had soon burned it to the ground. They had kept up a queer sort of powwow there for days that spring, killing two settlers and frightening all the others into taking refuge with the Jordans on Sunday Island. Flint had not been entirely open and aboveboard with Joel Sargent, they admitted. It was a risky business settling anywhere along the coast, but that point of land was notorious. There was something queer and sinister about it. The Indians held it in very peculiar regard. It must in some way be connected with their religion, for every year in the late spring they had appeared in hordes, ugly and resentful of the white men's intrusion.

"There was a man hereabouts who'd been captive in Canada and knew some of their language told us about it," Ethan explained. "He said 'twas called 'Passageewakeag' or some-such soundin' name that meant 'the place of ghosts or spirits.' That's why it maddens 'em to have settlers on it."

"Yes, it's got a bad name, that land has," the older Jordan put in. "I'd be the last to grudge helpin' newcomers out, but it's courtin' trouble to settle here. Take the islands now—there's still a plenty round about to be had for the squattin'."

"I want no island." Joel Sargent's mouth was set. "This here's my claim, an' here I mean to stay, Injuns or no Injuns."

" 'Tain't just you that'll be in danger," Jordan reminded him. "Remember the rest of us don't hanker to lose our scalps."

They talked of other matters after that, but a queer stiffness was on them all, as if even then Indians lurked behind the nearer trees of the clearing. When they turned to go back to their dory Seth Jordan spoke pleasantly to Dolly.

"My Aunt Hepsa lives along of us over to the Island," he told her. "She's past seventy, but smart's a whip. She'll be proud to have you pay her a visit."

So once again the Sargent family piled aboard the *Isabella B.* for the night. There was talk and discussion between the men and Dolly for many more hours. But Marguerite was too spent with the events of the day to pay much heed. She watched the light deepen into darkness

over the water, straining her eyes to see that line of far hills
as long as possible. Strange how they had laid hold of her,
those hills with their French name and rugged shapes. It
was heartening to see them next morning when she climbed
up from the cabin, and though she smiled at her own folly,
she hailed them in inward "Bonjour."

Already the men were at work in the woods higher up
from shore. Here the trees were taller and of a proper size
for building. Joel Sargent and Ira were busy with their axes
and cross-saws, and even Captain Hunt and Caleb had been
pressed into service. Their voices and the sound of ax blows
came clearly over the water. After a while they returned
to the vessel to rest and eat a meal of hasty pudding. They
were too tired to talk much, and Joel Sargent still wore the
grim expression of the day before so that none of the children dared approach him. After they had eaten, plans were
discussed for getting the animals ashore. The simplest way,
they all agreed, was to dump them over the side and let
them swim in.

"They'll make a straight wake for land every time," the
Captain assured them. "That calf's strong enough now, an'
the sheep will follow."

Marguerite, Dolly, and the younger children were all
put ashore in the small skiff. Joel and Captain Hunt went
back to their tree-chopping, leaving Ira and Caleb to land
the cattle. It was not so easy as they had expected. Marguerite and the children sat on a large rock near the beach
and watched the efforts of Ira and Caleb to get the animals
over the side. The sheep could be bundled over, though
they struggled and squirmed desperately, but old Brindle
was anything but manageable. It was necessary therefore

to put the sheep over first. They swam inshore bravely enough, though it took a deal of running about before Marguerite and the twins could catch and bring them, draggled and dripping, to the tethering place. At last Ira and Caleb, despairing of getting the cow overboard, hit upon the plan of dumping the calf in first. This had the desired effect. Once the calf struck the water with loud cries, its mother was easily pushed over the side after it. But unfortunately the calf, instead of swimming toward the cove, struck out in the opposite direction. The cow, being thoroughly frightened by this time and confused with the struggle on board the *Isabella B.*, seemed to lose all sense of direction and started swimming after her calf, both of them heading out into the open channel between shore and Sunday Island. The tide ran hard through there. It was well on the ebb, a fact which had been overlooked in taking this time for landing. Before the little group on shore could realize what had happened, a wide stretch of water showed between the pair and the boat. In spite of the iciness of the water they were swimming strong. Not only this, but in their flounderings as they went overboard, one of them had struck the dory tied alongside, overturning it and scattering the two pair of oars. Already Ira was letting himself down by the rope to right it again, but meantime old Brindle and her calf were making great headway.

"Oh, oh, they'll be drownded!" screamed the twins, jumping up and down wildly.

Their mother stared after the animals despairingly, unable to muster a word.

Marguerite could never be sure how she got into the

skiff. She must have run along the beach, for a pebble flew up and struck her smartly on the cheek. It was many months since she had had a pair of oars in her hands, but she reached for one without hesitation and standing upright in the stern summoned all her strength for pushing off. The skiff rocked under her, grated over the pebbles, and then slid into the water. A confusion of cries was in her ears from those on land and those aboard the vessel, but she shook her head and bent to the oars, only glancing over her shoulder every now and again for a sight of the tawny bobbing heads.

"Mon Dieu!" she murmured between set teeth, in a queer jumble of French and English. "They must not drown. Il faut les sauver!"

But it was no time to waste breath on heavenly petitions. She had need of all she could muster. Once she had the skiff headed out into the channel the tide would help, but the animals were also being swept along by it. Then the oars were clumsy affairs, made to fit a man's hands rather than her own thin brown ones. Nevertheless she gripped valiantly, bracing her bare feet against a wooden cleat till her toes ached with the pressure. Drops of sweat rose on her forehead and trickled down over her face. She felt them on her cheeks and lips as she tugged tirelessly at the oars.

Now it seemed that she was gaining on the two a little. Then a new fear struck her. Perhaps the cow and calf were growing weaker. Maybe she would not reach them before they sank in that cold, cold water. She redoubled her efforts and the little boat shot forward. A few moments more and she could see Brindle and her calf clearly, their brown heads well out of water and their eyes rolling and panic-stricken. Since she had no rope with which to make them fast, even had she been skillful enough to get it about their necks, she decided to try and head them in the direction of Sunday Island, which lay a quarter of a mile or so beyond. If they continued to make for the channel and open water nothing could save them. So she brought the skiff as close alongside as she could, even thumping the calf with an oar and calling out to them with what breath was left her.

The calf seemed nearly exhausted, and even old Brindle was swimming more slowly all the time.

"Here, Boss—here, Boss!" she called, imitating Caleb's manner as best she could and heading her bow towards the island. It seemed a long time before she saw to her relief that they were following her in. Ira and Caleb were now in the dory and would be there soon if only she could get the beasts safely into shallow water. Looking over her shoulder as she pulled she could see a cove, with a cleared field above it. Never had grass looked so green or beautiful to her.

And then old Brindle's brown shoulders reared themselves up from the water. That meant she had touched bottom. Another moment and Marguerite saw her struggling up the beach with the calf wobbling weakly after.

"Oh, mon Dieu!" she breathed. "Merci bien!" and she let herself slump over the oars.

She felt suddenly very weak and dizzy, and a queer ringing filled her ears as if gigantic seashells were pressed against them. She was only half aware of Ira Sargent, standing up to his waist in water dragging the boat inshore.

"They are safe?" she managed to ask him faintly as he half lifted her out and set her high and dry on a tangle of beach pea-vines.

"Yes," he told her. "I couldn't 've headed 'em in better myself. You just lay here a spell and get your wind back."

She closed her eyes obediently. The sun was warm on her lids, and her heart pounded less violently. She could hear Caleb calling, "Here, Boss—here, Boss" and the tide shuffling the pebbles farther down. She would have felt very well content had it not been for the aching of her back and shoulders.

And then she heard another voice mingled with Ira's, a woman's voice, high and lively as a bird's.

"Well, I never!" it said. "If I'd 'a known I was havin' visitors I'd 'a been down to meet ye."

Marguerite opened her eyes to see a little old woman approaching. As grotesque as a crooked apple tree decked out in print calico, the little figure bent over her, peering down with bright black eyes in nests of crisscross wrinkles.

"Mercy me," she went on, her head with its smoothly parted gray hair tilting to one side oddly, "you ain't an Injun, be ye?"

Marguerite smiled a little wanly, but Caleb was by to speak up.

"She's French," he said. "That's 'bout the same."

"Well, that's news to me," she answered, her face breaking up into innumerable fine lines of kindly merriment. "All the same, I guess some milk an' bread fresh out o' the pan wouldn't taste amiss after chasing those pesky critters all the way across. Oh, yes," she added, with another wag of her head, "I seen you from the house an' I lit out for shore quick's I could."

Presently Marguerite found herself following the little figure up a footpath. Her breath still came short and she ached all over, but she felt that if this stranger had asked her to mount a precipice, she would have tried to do her bidding.

"Hepsa Jordan, that's my name," she was telling them as they went towards the house in its square field. "I'm aunt to Seth and his son Ethan. Likely they told you."

She moved with a quickness that made the skirts of her print dress dip and billow about her ankles. Her feet stepped briskly in homemade slippers of cowhide as she led the way to the square-set house. With its wide boards of weathered gray and the sheds and outbuildings set so close, Marguerite thought it looked not unlike some gray old dam with her lambs. But it was the dooryard of gay flowers that made her breath come shorter, rather than the steep climb. It seemed nothing short of a miracle to find clove pinks, sunflowers, morning-glories, and even a cinnamon rose bush blooming in such a far place, and the girl's exclamations of wonder pleased the old woman mightily.

"Why, I wouldn't feel I was settled proper without I had me a garden of posies," she said. Then as she saw Marguerite marveling at the rose bush, she added with a smile, "I fetched that slip clear from Boston myself. Seth he vowed 'twouldn't catch on, but I knew better. It takes a dreadful lot to kill a rose bush."

"Like some folks, eh?" laughed Ira.

"That's the truth if you mean me," she answered him. "I was past seventy-three when I told Seth I'd come here, an' I ain't been ailin' a day since. That's my loom an' spinnin' wheel in the shed yonder. When we shear our sheep the wool's stored there an' it's there I dye an' spin an' do my weavin'. I've been a great hand at such work all my days. Seems a pity I've no woman person to help me with housework so I could keep at my weavin' an' patchin' an' herb-dryin'. Yes, I tell Ethan it's time he fetched home a wife."

Marguerite was to learn much that afternoon as they sat in the sunny kitchen eating warm cornbread from the pan just drawn out of the brick oven, drinking milk from pewter mugs that Aunt Hepsa said her mother's people had brought with them from Scotland. Even pleasanter than the food and quiet of the kitchen was the old lady's lively talk of herself and of their scattered neighbors.

"Seth he tells me you've fetched along a regular snarl of young ones," she said as she refilled their mugs, "an' I said I wished as how he'd helped himself to a few. Eliza and Sam Stanley have got three, but they're a good half-day's sail to the west o' your point. Then there's the Morses, Hiram an' Mary Jane. They're a young pair, lately settled over to the head o' Seal Cove with a year-old baby. They stayed over here with me when there was that Injun trouble in the spring. The Welleses they ain't so far to the east o' you, an' there's four o' them—Nathan an' Hannah an' Timothy an' Abigail. She's smart, Abby is, 'bout eighteen by this time."

"An' pretty into the bargain?" asked Ira with a laugh.

"You'd best ask Ethan that," she answered with a knowing nod. "He's over to their place every chance he can get, an' I doubt it's for visitin' with the old folks. Tim he's pleasant-spoken an' a good worker, but he's cross-eyed, poor fellow—born in the middle o' the week an' lookin' both ways for Sunday, that's how my mother used to call it."

They all laughed together over this, and a deep warmth and contentment settled over the kitchen. Marguerite sat in a happy daze, only half aware of the talk that flowed between the old woman and Ira. She felt as she had not felt since she and Grand'mère and Oncle Pierre had boarded that ship for the New World. She could not have explained it in words, but she felt that here was a place of enduring comfort; here were gray walls, pewter mugs, flowers as gay as those she had left across the water in Le Havre, and an old lady with kind, bright eyes whose knitting needles clicked in time to her own words.

But presently it was time to go. The two Jordans came in from the woods and hearing the tale of the cow and her calf volunteered to help Ira get them across the channel. It was plain from their manner that they still disapproved of the Sargents' settling on the point, but they were not ones to deny help to neighbors in need. With a little sigh Marguerite rose to go with them. She had almost reached the doorstep when Hepsa Jordan spoke up.

"Leave the girl here with me tonight," she said to Ira. "She's kind of beat-out chasin' those critters, an' Ethan shall fetch her back tomorrow."

Marguerite pressed her hands tight together lest she show too great an eagerness. She felt sure that if Joel and Dolly Sargent had been there such a suggestion would have been instantly dismissed, but Caleb had run on ahead and was out of hearing, and Ira might not make any objection. She could scarcely contain her joy when she heard him fall into the plan easily.

"You'd best call me Aunt Hepsa, same's the rest do," her hostess told her as they stood in the open door watching the boats set out with the cow in tow and the calf made fast in the dory. "I'm not one for puttin' on cornstarch airs. Bound-out Girl or no, it's all one to me so long's you smart an' sensible."

Marguerite flushed at these words. She was suddenly aware of her bedraggled dress with a great rent in the front breadth, of her disheveled hair, and her skin, tanned and grimy from all those days without soap and water. The old woman must have read her thoughts, for without more ado she led her back into the house and to a room across the entry. Here again the girl's eyes widened to see as fine a cherry bedstead, spread with sheets and patchwork quilts, as one could wish for, and a low chair by the small-paned window, with piece bag and sewing basket beside it.

"This here's my chamber," the old lady explained with pride. "Most folks would use it for a parlor, but Seth he wanted I should have the best. The bed I've had since I was married. I picked the feathers an' wove the sheets myself, an' the quilts are filled with wool from our own sheep. Now if you've a mind to wash yourself," she added, bringing out a heavy towel of bird's-eye weave, "here's a towel to dry you. That bucket's full o' water, an' I keep soft soap in the covered dish there."

Marguerite needed no urging. Once she was alone, she let her clothes slip to the floor. Then standing on a braided rush mat she began to rub herself all over with the soap and water. It felt soft and lathery to her skin, and the water came chill but very fresh and invigorating from the wooden bucket. As she splashed and rubbed her body dry on the rough cloth she felt renewed in some strange way. It was as if she had shed all the drudgery and humiliation as well as the grime of those past days. She sang as she rebraided her dark hair. Her voice came full and unabashed, there being none by to chide her for the French words.

"*Sur le pont d'Avignon*," she sang over and over as Oncle Pierre had taught her.

> *On y danse, on y danse.*
> *Sur le pont d'Avignon,*
> *On y danse, tout en rond.*

"It is a thousand pities," she thought as she slipped into her old linen again, "that I cannot also have fresh garments, but one may not have everything in this world, as Grand'-mère so often told me."

When the room was tidied and the soapy water emptied, she joined Aunt Hepsa, who was bending over a huge iron kettle in the weaving shed, where wool was piled just as it came from the sheep's backs and other hanks which had been dyed hung waiting for spinning. Here also stood a spinning wheel, and a sturdy wooden loom took up half the place along with a quilting frame and reel.

"This dye's got to be stirred twice a day till it comes," she explained as she bent over it with a stout stick, "an' where I'm to get the time to color all this wool an' spin it into cloth I don't know."

The midafternoon sun came in at the door, touching a hank of reddish yarn into a royal color. Marguerite stood amazed before the sight. In France she had seen weavers and lacemakers, but never such a place as this nor so strange a little figure as Hepsa Jordan made over the dye pot.

"If she were not so kind and I did not know better," she thought, "I should say she might be a witch."

"Supposin' we go up to the pasture a ways," the other

said after a little. "I've been meanin' to get me a basketful o' bay leaves for this long spell. They make the best fast yellow dye there is, an' I need aplenty to mix with that brown for Ethan's winter linsey."

So presently they were climbing a steep footpath that led among rocks and spruces to a higher patch of open green where sheep's backs and gray boulders were thickly scattered. Now and then a ram's bell sounded from some far thicket, and the sea thudded faintly along the outer ledges.

"It's a lovely island," Marguerite said. "I did not know it was so big."

"Yes, it's sightly," her companion agreed. "We landed on it a Sunday 'most ten years back. That's how it comes by the name. Seth an' Ethan they've been over it all, even when they had to cut a way through the tall woods, but I don't get so far from the house now it's built to my liking. If I had a young one about like you, I expect I'd scramble round more."

"You have no children of your own then?" Marguerite put the question timidly.

"No livin' ones. I buried two along with my man years back. Lost the lot of 'em in a spell o' the fever. But I helped Seth to raise Ethan, an' he's like my own."

They came into the pasture now, where the bayberry bushes were so green and springing that they must push their way between. Wherever they bruised them the leaves gave out a strong scent, very crisp and spicy. This was so delicious that Marguerite sniffed eagerly as if she had been a young colt turned out to pasture. Her blood tingled from her late scrubbing and the climb in sun and wind.

She felt light and nimble and alive with new wonder. Below her the ranks of firs and spruces went down to the shore in thickset green. She could see the Jordan house, with smoke at the chimney and a bit of color that she knew for the flowers in the dooryard. Off to the southwest there were the far lines of Fox and Deer islands, and across the channel waters the Sargents' cove and the *Isabella B.* at anchor. And farther away to the eastward more islands and the Mount Desert hills, faintly blue and rugged. Seeing them so, it was as if she knew herself for a part of all this miracle of land and sea and sky.

Though she could feel her feet firmly braced between the bayberry bushes of Sunday Island, Marguerite knew that something in her went out past the nearby ledges to those French hills and to the sea whose other shore was the world she had left behind.

Hepsa Jordan shaded her eyes with her hand and took her fill of the horizon line.

"I declare it does a body good to come up here once in a while," she said. "Some folks keep so close to their kitchen fires they wouldn't know if the sun was to set in the east someday. Here, child, take the basket and get me the topmost parts. We can strip the leaves off afterwards. I'm goin' on a ways to hunt a few mullein leaves. There's no better cure for some complaints than mullein leaves boiled in milk."

Marguerite sang once more as she filled the basket with fragrant bay. Sometimes at her approach a sheep would bleat or start away and at other times stand still, regarding her with foolish bright eyes. When the basket was heaped with green she went to join Aunt Hepsa, whose small figure and head in its neatly tied kerchief she could see above her on a bare ledge of rock that cropped out boldly. Smaller plants grew there, springing out of every crack and crevice, and some low bushes with flowers of a deep pinkish color.

"Sheep laurel," the old lady told her. " 'Tain't held so choice as the tall kind that grows in the hills, but I think it's pretty. I've heard it called Calico Bush in these parts, an' there's a ballad they sing of it."

Marguerite would have liked to hear it then and there, but Hepsa Jordan said it was too late. Maybe after supper, if Seth felt like scraping his fiddle strings, she would sing it for her. Marguerite wished they need never leave the pasture, but the time had come. So they retraced their steps, the girl chatting freely of herself, telling of Le Havre, of Grand'mère and Oncle Pierre, and of the embroidery lessons the Sisters in the convent had given her.

"It's a pity to have you forget such things in a place like this," the old woman said, "for there ain't likely to be much call for fancy stitches with all those young ones wearing the clothes off'n their backs an' a yard o' new cloth worth its weight in hard silver. First look I had at you I could tell you was raised more genteel than most. Young's you be, you've had more'n your share o' trouble, but you'll weather it. Yes, a young tree bends where an old tree breaks."

As they came through the woods the old woman's quick eye found a couple of late-blooming lady-slippers. These she added to the mullein leaves, explaining as she did so that the plant could be used for brewing a tea excellent for quieting the nerves of restless patients. It was evident, thought Marguerite, that her companion possessed more than a common store of such knowledge.

"There's an herb to cure 'most every ailment," she told the girl. "I will say this much for the Injuns—they've learned more from growin' plants than most doctors an' apothecaries I've met with in my time."

Marguerite thought the kitchen even pleasanter by fire and candlelight than before. The homemade bayberry drips gave out almost as fine a fragrance as the leaves she set to work stripping after the meal was over and the dishes washed. She said little, being somewhat in awe of Seth and Ethan, who took little heed of her presence. They were telling Aunt Hepsa of Joel Sargent's determination to settle on the point regardless of their warnings.

"Ain't goin' to move so much as a mile," Seth told her. "Means to build him a log house on that cellar an' won't take advice from no one. Any fool had ought to know this is no time to cut logs with the sap well in 'em, but he's commenced fellin' trees. 'You're in for trouble with 'em shrinkin',' I says to him, but 'twas only wastin' my breath."

Ethan was full of a plan for returning to Portsmouth with Captain Hunt on the *Isabella B.* He and Timothy Welles could work their way that far, returning in a sloop which they would tow.

"With the weather likely to hold through July we're pretty certain of a fair voyage back, an' it's a chance to lay in supplies."

But his father demurred, being loath to spare him from their crops just then. Besides, there was the fear of Indians for those who journeyed and those who stayed at home. However, he agreed to think the matter over before Captain Hunt made arrangements to leave.

"If you do go, Ethan," Aunt Hepsa spoke up, "there's just one thing you can fetch me back an' that's some indigo.

I can find makeshift dyes for the other colors, but you can't set a blue pot without you have indigo."

"Ain't there colors enough besides that you must have blue?" Ethan asked her smiling.

"For the most o' my patchwork, yes," she answered. "But you know I've been hankerin' to piece me a quilt o' that 'Delectable Mountains' pattern. I'd sooner make none at all if I can't have it blue an' buff accordin' to my fancy."

"Well, that bein' so," Ethan said, "I suppose I'll have to fetch you a bag o' indigo if I have to hunt it from door to door!"

He had a slow, good-natured smile that suited his broad frame and heavy, dark brows. Marguerite liked him, but not so well as Ira. Presently at his aunt's bidding Seth brought out his fiddle and tightened the strings. Marguerite caught her breath with excitement at the first scraping of the bow along them. She had not heard a fiddle for so long—not since Oncle Pierre's had followed him to the bottom of the sea. Somehow it seemed even more extraordinary to hear it in this far-off place, at the edge of the wilderness and already echoing to Indian alarms. Seth Jordan did not play so well as Oncle Pierre; his fingers were stiff and one of his strings was missing. Still, any sort of melody seemed good to Marguerite, and the ballad she was to hear was certainly as sad as all such tales of lost or blighted love should be.

"Aunt Hepsa she used to be a great hand at singin' in her young days," Ethan had told their guest under cover of the noise made by the fiddle-tuning. "She knows a lot besides 'Calico Bush.' "

And then the old woman folded her hands in her lap and began in a voice that was still sweet, though quavering on the higher notes. Not once till the end did she pause or falter for a single word. Marguerite listened intently, fearful lest some of the English phrases should be unfamiliar to her.

> Calico, sprigged calico,
> My love, Judy, she plagued me so
> For a weddin' dress of calico
> That off to Portsmouth I must go,
> Twenty miles in a storm of snow.
> > *Calico, sprigged calico!*

> O, Judy, what for would you have me go
> So far an' wide in a northeast blow?
> The Parson will wed us as true, I know,
> In patches as in sprigged calico.

> But she shook her head and she wouldn't take "no,"
> For her heart it was fixed on calico,
> On calico, sprigged calico.
> While she by the fire did bend and sew
> Off I set, for I loved her so,
> Too well to lose her to black-eyed Joe
> All for the want of calico,
> > *Of calico, sprigged calico!*

> The snow it fell and the winds did blow.
> I wandered high and I wandered low
> Till night came on me black as a crow,
> And never a light did shine or show,
> > *Calico, sprigged calico!*

I laid me down where the laurels grow,
All spent with the cold and the falling snow.
"O, Judy," I cried in deepest woe,
"Cursed be our love and calico,
    Calico, sprigged calico!"

'Twas Spring before they found me so,
Dead and perished from top to toe.
Tears from my Judy's eyes did flow,
"O cruel pride that laid him low,
"My true love's died for calico,
    For calico, sprigged calico!"

So, maids who pass where the laurels grow,
Think on this tale of long ago.
Set not your hearts on a furbelow
Lest you live to curse sprigged calico,
    Calico, sprigged calico!

There was silence in the kitchen after the song ended. Then Ethan broke it as he rose to climb to his room aloft.

"He was a plumb fool to go, that fellow was," he muttered. "I say it served him right to get froze."

"But he loved her so," sighed Marguerite contentedly. "And it is necessary that a ballad should be sad."

"Well, all I know is my voice ain't what 'twas," Aunt Hepsa remarked with a nod. "It's goin' same way as my cashmere shawl—kind o' thin in spots. Come along to bed, child."

Marguerite followed her into the bedroom. Soon she was beside her under the covers of the wide old bed, her mind a queer jumble of islands and water, colored wools, pasture herbs, and plaintive ballad airs.

Next morning when she took leave of Aunt Hepsa a bond had sprung up between them, though the girl's thanks were awkward and faltering, and the old woman's parting words were almost equally so.

"Well, good-by, Maggie," she called after her from the door. "You can come again when you've got a mind to."

PART 2 FALL

It was the first day of September on the calendar that Ira Sargent had made by cutting a notch for each day that passed on a pole beside the door-step. But even without that and the sight of the nearly completed log house and cornfield, Marguerite thought she would have known that summer was over. Goldenrod and red berries would have told her; a deeper haze on the Mount Desert hills, and the incessant chirping of crickets morning, noon, and night.

"Rubbin' their hind legs together, that's how they do it," the twins had explained to her the evening before as they went to sleep on the spruce boughs of their makeshift shelter.

But there was little time to discuss crickets and their like that morning, for it was to be a great day, one on which all their thoughts had been bent for many weeks past.

"Well, it's turned out fair for the Raisin'," Dolly Sargent had announced almost before the sun was fully up from the water, "for which I'm thankful. When I heard the wind commence to blow last night I declare my heart 'most failed me thinkin' it might storm to keep the folks from comin'."

"An' Captain Hunt delayed again," added her husband as he built up a fire in the rough oven of beach stones.

62

Marguerite was as eager as the children for the activity to begin. She had never heard of a Raising, and Caleb had been more than usually scornful in consequence.

"How'd you think we'd get the roof on 'fore frost," he had demanded, "without we had some help? It's took Pa an' Ira an' me an' the Cap'n 'most all summer to get the logs cut an' dragged down here an' part set up. I tell you, women folks don't know nothin' when it comes to buildin' houses."

But it was from Ira and the little girls that Marguerite learned more. A roof-raising seemed to be in the nature of a celebration, from all she could gather. Neighbors might disapprove of things one did and said, but when the time came to put the roof on one's house they would come to help. It was a duty, and also an excuse for festivity. So they would all be coming soon—the Jordans from Sunday Island; the Stanley family from the west; the Welleses from the east, and the Morses with their baby from Seal Cove. That was to be eventful enough, without the sailing of the *Isabella B.*, but Captain Hunt had said he would be off once

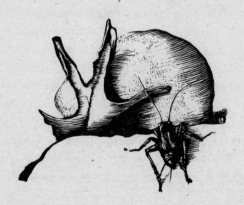

the roof was laid on. Twice he had been set to go. Once Timothy Welles was laid up with a swollen hand, and then there had been a rumor of Indians to delay them. Ethan and Timothy were to go with him as far as Portsmouth, where he would readily find others to sail to Boston. Already the two young men had been entrusted with various commissions to bring back in their sloop—food supplies, farm tools, cloth, and other necessities.

"I expect they won't start till their own chores are done," said Dolly, who was already busy over her stores of meal and milk and the cheese she and Marguerite had made yesterday.

Caleb was out in the dory fishing. They could see his orange head bent over the side as he worked his lines skillfully. Caleb was a great hand at fishing. Already he had long strings of cod and haddock drying for winter use. "A likely boy," Hepsa Jordan had said of him. " 'Course you can't expect too much when they're between the hay an' grass same's he is, but I'll lay he'll turn out smarter 'n the Stanleys' Andrew."

Marguerite had not yet seen Andrew, but she certainly hoped he would be more kindly disposed to her than Caleb. She and the twins were helping to pick feathers from several fine wildfowl the Captain and Ira had shot for the feast, while Jacob and Patty ran to and from bringing wintergreen and partridge berries for garnishing. Near at hand Debby kicked and gurgled in the wooden cradle set out on the mossy ground. Every now and again Marguerite paused in her work to set the rockers in motion or to make sure the child did not wriggle free of the shawl's worn folds. The air came crisp from the northwest, and Debby was wearing her best cotton dress in honor of the Raising, not the usual one of heavy holland that did her for every day. Her little face was almost as sunburned as the older children's, her hair bleached white as theirs.

"She'll be the smallest one at the Raisin', I guess," said Becky, "littler 'n the Morses' baby if they fetch him."

" 'Course they'll fetch him," Susan told her with scorn. "They'd never leave him home for the Injuns to get, maybe."

"Mercy sakes, don't talk of Injuns today," chided Dolly from the rough log table set in the open where she was stirring cornmeal in the largest iron kettle. "I've got enough on my hands without worryin' over that. Besides, it's temptin' Providence when they've kept away from these parts all summer."

Dolly Sargent appeared almost happy with the prospect of visitors so near at hand. She had donned her best calico and a clean kerchief and had found some bits of the blue yarn to tie Marguerite's braids and the twins' yellow pigtails.

"Wisht I had somethin' clean to put on Jacob's back an' Patty's," she sighed as they came running back with their hands full of the red berries, their faces smeared, and their hair stuck full of twigs and burrs. "I'll help finish with these feathers, Maggie. You take 'em up to the spring for a scrubbin'. Get a cloth from the chest, an' the comb an' shears, for you'll have to cut out all those burrs. I can't have folks sayin' my young ones look like a pair o' sheep fetched in from pasture!"

There had been precious little time for washing and combing in all those weeks, so the task of making them presentable was not easy. Marguerite, however, was not one to give up readily.

"If I had soap I should not have to rub so hard," she told the protesting pair as she dipped the spring water up by the gourdful, pouring it over their hands and faces and then polishing away with the rough linen towel.

"You've took my skin off a'ready!" cried Patty.

"An' my nose!" put in Jacob, who had turned as red as the rock maple growing near the little spring.

Their hair presented even greater difficulties. It was no use trying to drag a comb through, and when she had cut out all snags and burrs the effect was worse than before.

"Ciel!" she exclaimed, laughing in spite of herself. "But you look as if the mice had been nibbling at you."

Marguerite watched the two run off to join the others, glad that they could not see how queer they looked. She lingered a moment or so to bathe her own face with the cool water and to smooth her hair. After she had done so a sudden curiosity overcame her to see herself again. She had almost forgotten what her face was like in those long, busy days of hard work.

She knelt on the moss that grew about the spring, waiting for the water to clear of the ripples she had made in it. A leaf from the rock maple drifted down to settle on the surface like a tiny flame. Motionless it lay there on the dark water so that when she peered in and saw herself at last the leaf seemed to be caught in her own hair. She saw it clearly beside the paler oval of her face, as much a part of her as the dark eyes and the teeth that showed white between her lips. And suddenly, as she stared, this nose and mouth, this pointed chin and eyes and parted hair that she knew for her own, all seemed very strange to her. It was as if she looked at the picture of a girl she did not know. She shivered and sprang up with a quick catch of breath. Was it only the red leaf's doing, she wondered, or could people be such strangers to themselves?

As she sped down towards shore she heard Caleb calling from the cove. The twins ran to her, signaling excitedly that the boats were coming. Sure enough a triangular patch of sail was putting out from Sunday Island, and another was making its way round the eastern point.

"They're a-comin', Maggie!" Becky was shouting.

"Quick," cried Susan, seizing her hand, "let's go to meet 'em."

It seemed nothing short of a miracle to see so many people flocking to their point. Marguerite counted each of the four boatloads over as its occupants set foot on the beach. First there were the three from Sunday Island, Aunt Hepsa's old face wrinkled with pleasure over the covered basket of good things she had brought for the feast. Next came the Morses—Hiram, Mary Jane, and Reuben the baby; with Eliza and Sam Stanley and their three sturdy children appearing from the other direction in a stout dory, rowed by Sam and shock-headed young Andrew. Last of all there were the Welleses, Timothy sailing his sister Abigail in the sloop which he and Ethan were to tow to Portsmouth, and their parents, Nathan and Hannah, following in a smaller rig. Marguerite was curious to set eyes on Abby Welles, and so she guessed must Ira be, for he had been the first on hand to help her step ashore, with Ethan close on his heels. No, Marguerite decided, Aunt Hepsa had not said too much of this girl's charms. She looked very pretty in her full cotton dress that was almost as deep a pink as the flowers of the calico bush. Under the sunbonnet she wore, her cheeks showed warm and softly rounded, her eyes a quiet gray, and her hair brown and curling at either side of the parting. She stepped lightly over the stones in her homemade slippers of cowhide bound with thongs about her ankles. Seeing her fresh dress and white knitted stockings, Marguerite hung back, more than ever conscious of her own bare feet and the dingy, bedraggled holland dress she had already half outgrown. But Aunt Hepsa was beckoning.

"Here, Maggie," she said, feeling about in the depths of the calico workbag she had brought. "See if these stockings fit you. I presume likely you won't get time to knit none for yourself against cold weather."

Marguerite's hands trembled as she unrolled the stockings, marking how firm and close they were knit of gray wool with a border of red yarn at the top.

"Ah, merci bien," she cried, reverting to her French as she still did in moments of emotion. "They are beautiful. I shall be most proud to wear them."

"There now, child, it's nothin'. Go set this basket in a shady spot where the butter pat won't run."

Marguerite would have liked to help roast the fowl and set out the food with the women, but she was soon detailed to watch over the children.

"Keep those young ones well out o' the men's way, Maggie," Dolly charged her. "Can't have any under foot for a log to fall on 'em or a hand chopped off, maybe."

Kate Stanley was tow-haired and square, a stolid child of nine, while her younger brother William was a freckled scamp of a boy two years younger. They followed the young Sargents as Marguerite, with Debby in her arms, led the way to a point just east of the new house. Here Joel had set up a stout pole that had been used with rope for hauling stones from the beach. The little group settled themselves about it now to watch the men at work.

"My, look how they heft the logs," exclaimed Becky, "as easy as if they was little sticks!"

"One, two, three, four, five," counted Susan method-ically on her fingers, "six, seven, eight, an' the Cap'n makes nine. I never see nine whole men a-workin' all to once in my life."

"That's my pa with the biggest ax," Kate pointed out. "He can make the chips fly 'most over to here."

"An' that's my Uncle Ira over there on the ladder!" put in Jacob proudly. "He's climbed up highest."

Marguerite watched in fascination as the figures of the men moved to and fro in the strong September sunshine. They lifted and laid the great brown logs in place so surely and swiftly. Only now and again one was too heavy or rebellious for them, or another slipped as they tugged and raised it. That made her know how hard they were straining to set them one upon another with the notched ends fitting into corners according to the pattern. It was a wonder to see the upper framework mounting miraculously under their efforts, while their bare backs and shoulders glistened with sweat.

"Mon Dieu," she thought to herself, "but it is a fine thing to be a man and turn trees into houses!"

"We've got boards in our house," Kate was telling the twins. "Our pa he fetched them from the sawmill way up

the inlet. He says a log house ain't no kind for decent folks. I heard him tell my ma so last night."

"Well, we'll have a board one too someday," Susan hastened to assure her. " 'Twasn't our fault the Injuns burned the other house up."

"They'll do it again maybe," suggested the practical Kate. "My pa he thinks your folks are plumb foolish to build it here."

"Yes," her brother added, "Injuns are likely to come again an' bring trouble on us all."

But in another moment a shout went up from the men. The first log was being laid on the roof.

Then it was time for them all to gather round the log table where the six women had spread their feast. Marguerite's eyes widened to see so much food after their fare of fish and meal and berries. Here were smoked meats, fowl, and eggs, new corn and beans, stewed pumpkin and turnips, and butter and wild honey to flavor the cornbread and hasty pudding. She ran about at Dolly Sargent's bidding, now fetching wooden plates heaped with food to the men who had flung themselves on the ground nearby; now quieting the children with good things or hurrying up to the spring for a bucket of fresh water. Or again she sat herself down among the children, scarcely able to eat for the wonder of looking from face to face of all those gathered about the table. She felt a queer beat of happiness within her, seeing them all so hearty and full of life and good nature. Sometimes she even dared to smile into one of the men's or women's faces, and when Abby Welles returned her look with a show of friendliness she tingled with pleased excitement. Surely, she thought, as she spread a slab of johnnycake thick with honey for Jacob, surely it is a fine thing to have a Raising.

Talk flowed freely all about her, and easy laughter such as she had not heard for many months. Only now and again, if someone said the word "Indian," was there a sudden silence or eyes turned quickly to the edge of the woods. In spite of her wrinkles Hepsa Jordan appeared the gayest and most carefree of them all. The strings of her dark sunbonnet wagged continually as she nodded her head or made quick retort.

"I declare," she said beaming upon them all, "I ain't had so much sociability since I can remember. Seth he was dreadful afraid we were in for a spell o' fog when the wind turned, but I told him I knew better, for only the day before I'd dropped a knife an' it stuck in point-first. That's a sure sign of company. I never knew it to fail."

"She's got a sure sign to fit everythin'," laughed her nephew. "I wouldn't dast to do my plantin' without she told me the moon was set in the right quarter."

"An' she's right, Seth Jordan," spoke up Hannah Welles. "You men maybe think it's all your doin' that the crops thrive, but there's a lot to havin' the moon on your side as well."

"Well, I ain't sayin' as I'd swap Hepsa for all the rest of you put together," Seth answered, "not even for Abby there that's a sight for sore eyes."

"Land, Seth," Hepsa laughed, "you talk plain foolish. What would a girl like Abby want with signs an' brewin's? That for old folks like me. Still," she added with another headshake, "I can see as far into a stone wall as the next person, if I do say so."

Abby had blushed a rosy color at such personal remarks. She sat between Ira and Ethan, her pink skirts spread daintily about her on the moss. She said little, but her eyes were softly bright as she listened to the talk about her and sometimes, when either of her neighbors addressed to her in a low voice some remark not meant for the rest of the company, a dimple would deepen in one of her cheeks. Marguerite watched fascinated to see it come and go. It would be nice, she thought, to wear a pink calico dress and white stockings and to sit between two young men in just such a way.

"Come, Maggie," Dolly Sargent broke in on her thoughts, "finish your food and help me clear up what's left."

But Hepsa Jordan rose instead.

"Let the girl be for a bit," she said. "I'll give you a hand with the things. She'd ought to eat more an' fatten up some," she added, giving Marguerite's sharp shoulderblades a tap as she went by. "Why, she's so thin she'd have to stand up twice to make a shadow."

After the men had lolled a while longer, they returned to their work. Axes and hammers rang out with even greater vigor, and the roof took shape amazingly before their eyes. Caleb and Andrew clambered about at the men's bidding, carrying tools and nails, and whistling and shouting to give vent to their own feelings of importance. The women gathered in a little group about the cleared log table and spread out their knitting or patchwork, giving an occasional rock to Debby's cradle or wrapping the Morse baby into his shawl. Marguerite would have liked to stay with them to watch Abby's pretty ways and to hear

Aunt Hepsa's talk, but she knew this would not be encouraged. Her place was to keep the children from under foot.

But it was not so easy to keep them amused. The twins and Kate Stanley quarreled over the corncob doll and succeeded in tearing its calico dress. William cut his finger whittling a toy boat, and Jacob and Patty kept straying toward the log house whenever Marguerite so much as turned her back. Pumpkin, the dog, who usually slept after a meal of any sort, seemed upset by so many strangers. He ran sniffing about, barking in short, excited yelps and generally making a nuisance of himself.

"He's barking his 'afraid' barks," Becky said. "Maybe he smells Injuns."

Marguerite refused to belive this, but all the same he acted restless and made short dashes in the direction of the spring.

"Let's follow him a ways," urged William Stanley. "We can run real quick if we see anything."

Thinking that there could be no harm in a short sally, Marguerite agreed, and they set off together, the dog ahead. Suddenly, just as they came in sight of the spring, the hair along his back began to rise. He uttered a deep growl and stood uncertainly in the path. All eyes followed the direction of his sniffing nose. And there before them a great black bear was helping himself from a butter firkin left to cool.

He seemed bigger than a mountain to the children when he rose on his hind legs at their approach. His forepaws, dripping with butter, showed claws cruelly sharp and long. For what seemed like an endless space, rather than the few seconds which it must have been, the bear regarded them intently, making a deep rumbling of disapproval. The dog was edging forward now, growling fiercely and getting ready to spring. It was this which brought Marguerite to her senses.

"He'll be killed!" she said aloud and made a grab at the rough hair about Pumpkin's neck. But it slipped through her fingers.

The bear had dropped to all fours now and was coming toward them. He moved deliberately on his clumsy paws; still he came on, with an ugly look and red tongue showing.

"Quick, run quick!" Marguerite heard her own voice crying to the children and then, almost before she had time to think what she was doing or why, she had darted forward and caught up a wooden bucket left standing beside the spring. Fortunately she had filled it earlier, for there would not have been time to dip it full before the bear was upon her. As it was she found herself looking into the little yellow slits of bright eyes and it seemed to her she could even feel the heat of its breath. Then she gathered all her strength and hurled the bucket. The water struck full in the bear's face, splashing in a shower from the dark fur. Marguerite waited for nothing after that. She turned and fled, with only one look over her shoulder to make sure he was not plunging after them.

But he was not. With a bellow of disgust the bear turned and made for the woods, where even Pumpkin made no attempt to follow.

The children burst screaming into the clearing, telling an incoherent tale of the encounter. All the men stopped work and seized their muskets. They hurried up to the edge of the woods but soon returned empty-handed.

"Must have been a big fellow by the paw prints," Seth told them. "But he's gone now an' no mistake. Didn't leave much of your butter either, Hepsa."

"Bear meat makes good eatin'," said Andrew Stanley regretfully.

"Wisht we'd seen him first," added Caleb. "We'd 'a' had more sense 'n to scare him away." He gave a frown in Marguerite's direction.

"But we couldn't shoot him without any gun," Susan reminded him, "an' he was comin' right down after us."

"I guess *you* wouldn't have gone up close an' emptied the water on him, Caleb Sargent," retorted Becky.

Joel Sargent set his musket down again and reached for his hammer. "You done the right thing, Maggie," he said shortly.

"Yes," put in Dolly. "You had the children to think of."

"Got spunk for three times her size, that girl has," Hepsa Jordan was saying with an approving nod. Marguerite could not help feeling a little guilty. Perhaps she ought to explain that she had not thought much about what she was doing till it was over. Besides, if she had not been careless about leaving the butter and water bucket there she could not have done what she did; she was surprised that no one thought to chide her for this in the commotion. However, she was glad they had not. She found it altogether pleasant to be the object of praise.

Now the roof was laid on and only the smaller tasks such as cutting doors and windows, stuffing the chinks between logs, and the hammering and sawing of inside parts, remained to be done. Here was work enough for all. Even the younger children fetched baskets of moss to be stuffed into every crack and crevice, while Caleb and Andrew brought mud from up the inlet to pack in and harden.

Marguerite helped the children gather moss from the edge of the woods. It was pleasant to pull it up by the handful and to look back at the log house with the men clambering all over it and the women below in their full dresses and bonnets; pleasant to hear the sound of voices and hammering. She could make out the pink of Abby Welles' dress, like a calico flower.

"Abby Welles is pretty," she said to the little girls as they filled their baskets.

"Ethan Jordan's sweet on her," Kate Stanley told them. "Ma says she wouldn't wonder if he was to bring her something real handsome when he comes back from Portsmouth."

"I would that I were eighteen," sighed Marguerite, "and not bound-out any more."

"But you wouldn't look like her even then," reminded Susan. "She's got curls an' pink cheeks."

Remembering the dark face that had looked back at her from the mirror of the spring earlier that day, Marguerite knew she spoke the truth.

"If a girl ain't pretty then she's got to be extra good," Kate Stanley went on. "My ma says you won't get married no other way."

So they turned back to join the rest, chatting as they went.

How the accident happened Marguerite never could be sure, and those who were nearby each had a different story to tell. All of them had gathered about Joel Sargent who was fitting the precious panes of glass into two window frames he had made. Twelve little squares he had brought with him on the *Isabella B.* in case of need, so there could be but one narrow window to light each of the two rooms. He had leaded them together carefully, three rows of two panes each, and one was already in place to the right of the door.

"Steady there," he called to Ira who was helping him, "while I take off a bit of the sill."

Whether it was his hacking or Caleb's clambering to the roof at that moment that jarred the hammer out of place no one could say. But it came hurtling down directly above the door. Jacob, all intentness over the window, caught it full force, and tumbled to the doorstep with a sudden cry. Blood spurted from a gash on his forehead, and slowly widened into a reddish stain on the stone before there was even time to pick him up. For a moment it seemed he must be killed, what with all the blood and his going suddenly limp before them.

Then Hepsa Jordan was taking command of the situation. Marguerite found herself holding Jacob's head in her lap, helping to wash away the blood with some clean scraps of cloth from the bag the old lady had brought.

"There, he ain't hurt bad," she was reassuring Dolly and the rest. "Struck him too high for harm, but an inch or so nearer the temple an' I couldn't 'a' done much. Hold this cloth, Maggie, while I get out my sewin' things."

"What you goin' to do to him?" Dolly Sargent's eyes were frightened as she watched the old woman threading a needle.

"I got to stitch it together. 'Twon't heal no other way," she answered quietly. "Take your two hands, child," she ordered Marguerite, "an press the edges close as you can.

He'll be comin' round in a minute an' I want to get this over with. You, Caleb, fetch me some sea-water. I'll need that next."

Although Marguerite's hands felt cold as if they did not belong to her, she deftly followed the old woman's bidding. She was acutely aware of everything before her, of the white bone that showed under the oozing blood, and of the torn skin being drawn together. But although she saw the red staining her own fingers and felt the heaviness of Jacob's head, she seemed detached and far away. It was as if she were looking on at some picture of a hurt child and people tending it.

"Press harder," she heard Aunt Hepsa saying. "There's just one more stitch."

Things grew rather blurred after that. The blood pounded in her own temples and it was only Jacob's crying that roused her. Pain and salt water were bringing him to his senses again. Marguerite tried to ease him as Hepsa Jordan bathed and bandaged.

"There now," she was saying. "That's aplenty for now. He'll be good as new in a week. I'll send Seth over with some ointment to rub on. Why, Maggie, you're 'most as white's he is. Don't you go an' keel over after helpin' me out like an' old hand!"

"He had a mighty close shave, that young one did," Marguerite heard Hannah Welles remarking to Mary Jane Morse a little later when Jacob had been laid in a shady spot, well wrapped in one of the quilts. "But it's no kind of beginnin' for any house."

"Yes," the other agreed with a headshake. "Blood on the doorstep 'fore they've even moved in looks bad to me!"

"Oh, gracious," Abby broke in, her pretty face aghast,

"I wisht you wouldn't talk so. It fair gives me the creeps, it does."

"Signs are signs, Abby Welles," her mother rejoined, "an' I've seen too many in my time to overlook 'em. I tell you, I wouldn't set up to live in that house, after this, if you was to offer me a hundred pound sterling an' six china teacups."

"I'd do a heap for china teacups," sighed Abby.

"Well, it's temptin' Providence just the same," said her mother, "an' Hepsa Jordan she give me a queer look when that hammer struck him. She knows it don't mean no good, for all she kept her mouth shut."

Marguerite was glad Dolly had not been by to hear them. Their words made her uneasy, as talk of signs and portents always did. It was like being sent into a dark cellar alone to fetch something. She felt relieved when the word went round that it was nearly time for the *Isabella B.* to haul up her anchor.

Already Captain Hunt was aboard seeing to his ropes and sails, while Timothy Welles waited impatiently on the beach for Ethan to join him. But Ethan had run back to have another word with Abby. Marguerite could see them standing together a little way off, Abby's full pink skirts blown against his seaboots and rough breeches. The sound of her laugh came clear and bell-like before he ran down the beach to the dory and they pushed off. Andrew Stanley and Caleb were at the oars, all importance at being allowed to row them out. It was late afternoon now; the sun came slantwise over the water, making the seaweeds at the high-tide line ruddy, turning the *Isabella B.'s* mast from dull brown to tawny orange. Even her sail, patches and all, brightened as it filled.

Now the two boys were rowing back in the dory alone. The sloop with reefed canvas was made fast, and the little group on shore could see the figures of the three men busy with ropes and anchor chain.

"Tide's 'most full," Seth Jordan was saying. "They'll take the channel easy with this favoring wind."

"The Cap'n he's been hankerin' to be off for weeks," Joel Sargent told him. "He only stayed to oblige me with all this buildin'."

"Yes," his wife added, "an' I don't know where we'd have been but for his help. It makes me feel real bad to see the last of him."

"Oh, maybe not the last," Ira reminded her.

"You can't tell these days," she answered soberly. "I'd feel a heap easier in my mind with him by."

"Look, Maggie," Becky put in. "The anchor's up. She's headin' out."

Marguerite could understand Dolly's feelings as she stood watching the water widen between shore and this vessel that had been like home to them all. Even after the shelter had been built they had returned to the boat again and again. She knew every knothole and peg of its timbers, and the patches on its sail were as familiar to her as those on the quilt that covered Jacob.

"Good-by! Good-by!" the group on the point called as the vessel swung about.

"Good-by! Good-by!" the men called back, their voices crossing those coming over the water to them, so that the words became suddenly a single cry.

"I wish I was goin' too." Abby Welles spoke up.

"I'm glad you ain't," Ira answered at her side.

Marguerite's heart beat queerly to see the *Isabella B.*

slipping past their point. Already she looked small and strange, not the vessel they had known so well. Soon the dark trees on the farther headland would shut her from their sight. She ran with the twins and Patty to a boulder that she might keep the sight as long as possible. The sail showed very bright in the setting sun, and already the prow was heading out between the islands. Suddenly Marguerite was reminded of the Captain's words on their first morning out of Marblehead: "It takes you places without waitin' for no road." That was what he had said of the sea, and it was the truth. Once again she saw it as a watery highway going round and round the world, and once more she quickened to the fancy.

"There, it's gone," she heard one of the women say.

"Our cove looks dreadful empty without the *Isabella B.*," said Susan.

"Yes," echoed Becky. "I'm lonesome for her a'ready, ain't you, Maggie?"

That night, after their visitors had rowed away and the remains of the feast were eaten, they all turned into the new house. It was still unfinished inside, with a floor to be laid and beds and benches to be built against the walls. But logs burned on the hearth, the firelight shining on the rough stones that had so painstakingly been carried from the beach. The chimney rose in the center of the house, dividing the two rooms and making a fireplace for each.

Marguerite and the twins slept in the kitchen on make-shift beds, while Joel and his wife and the three younger children were in the other. A loft above housed Caleb and Ira, who climbed to it by means of a ladder. All this was still unfinished, but a roof at least was over them, and even

Dolly admitted that was a great step forward. Marguerite tossed on her spruce boughs. She found sleep long in coming, with the light of the dwindling fire making strange shadows on logs and rafters. She had grown used to sleeping in the half-open shelter, and the new quarters added to all the events of the day made her wakeful.

Jacob wailed from the other room, and hearing him she was reminded again of Hepsa Jordan drawing together the edges of that ugly gash. She saw it all plainly in her mind's eye, and inwardly she went over each gesture. Would she be able to do such a thing someday, she wondered? And suppose the hammer had hit him lower? What then? She shivered and huddled closer to the sleeping twins under the quilt folds. A strange bird called from the woods, and crickets were all about the house with their clamorings. Some night they would be still, and that would mean frost and winter almost upon them. She had heard Eliza Stanley say so to Hannah Welles only that afternoon. It was sad about crickets and the frost. Oncle Pierre had once sung her a little song about that. She must try to remember the words. Queer how her French ones were slipping away from her! It was easy to forget when she must keep them hidden as she did the ring and button round her neck. Her hands felt for them in the darkness.

She awoke to sunshine coming through the six small panes of window glass and all the unstuffed chinks. Caleb and Ira were stirring above, and Joel Sargent had already begun building up the fire. Marguerite sprang up and, slipping her dress quickly over her cotton underbody, was soon helping to stir the kettle of hasty pudding. The house would be full of hammering that day as she well knew.

So it was for all the week following and the one after that. Marguerite's feet were never still as she ran from spring to doorstep; from beach to garden patch and back a score of times a morning. The corn and turnips had not fared so badly for so late a planting, but the potatoes were poor and rotting. Every one must be gathered and stored away for winter use. The children and Marguerite grubbed over and over the bit of cleared land lest they overlook a single one of the precious brown lumps. Sometimes Caleb allowed them to turn his fish drying in the sun, and often he let Marguerite take a hand at the corn-grinding, which he had learned to do Indian-fashion with stones and wooden mallets. It was a wearisome task that made the muscles ache and the head throb if one kept at it long. But Marguerite never dared let Caleb know when she lagged. He would be sure to jeer, and though sometimes it seemed that he was less ready than of old to pounce upon her every failing, still she could not risk incurring his disfavor.

Jacob's hurt was almost healed, though the scar still showed red and jagged on his forehead and he liked to keep closer to Marguerite than had been his habit. Between him and Debby, who had reached the creeping stage, the girl had her hands full.

"Acts kind of pindling since he got that blow," Aunt Hepsa Jordan said one day when she came over on a short visit. "I'm goin' to bring over a brew o' my goldenrod tea to make him spruce up."

Seth had rowed her over along with some apples from his orchard. With Joel Sargent he went over to examine the applegrafts he had helped Flint make two springs before on some thornbushes in the clearing. These had been cut down and the apple shoots set in before the sap rose. Several of the grafts were doing well. Marguerite marveled to hear him talk of fruit from these apple cuttings. She and the children watched in fascination while he told how it must be done.

"Thorn trees are pretty tough wood," he was saying, "an' if these pippin shoots catch hold you'll have as good an apple tree as any up an' down the coast."

"That thornbush won't know itself when it commences to bear," laughed Ira as he turned to with his strong brown hands.

"And will they grow?" Marguerite asked incredulously. "Will there really be apples there sometime?"

"If we have luck," Seth told her, "an' the sap comes up good again next spring."

"It is wonderful," she murmured, "like magic."

"Well, I don't know about that, child," Hepsa Jordan said, "though come to think of it there's a wonder to anythin' that lives an' thrives."

"When the first fruits are gathered," Marguerite found herself grown quite voluble with the old lady by to listen, "we must remember to thank the tree. Often I have heard Grand'mère say so to make sure it will bear again."

"That's a good one," grinned Ira, "thankin' a tree."

"I've heard o' queerer doin's in my time," Hepsa retorted. "But 'twon't be for a good spell, to judge from the looks."

They walked together back to the house. The children must show her every corner of it and how their father was going to make a corner cupboard and shelves as soon as he had finished the shed to house Brindle and her calf. The sheep had been given to Seth Jordan in exchange for some pieces of wooden planking, a bag of nails, a keg of molasses, more cornmeal, and half of the next pig he killed. In addition Aunt Hepsa had agreed to spin and weave their wool into cloth for winter wear.

" 'Twon't be near enough for the yards you'll need," she had told Dolly, "but I never was one to stint a neighbor. You can send Maggie an' the twins over to help me set up the loom and pick the wool, an' we'll call it even."

The afternoom was unusually warm for mid-September, and there was an even greater color and shine on every leaf and grass blade. Dolly came out to sit beside Hepsa Jordan on the doorstep, and the children gathered on the ground roundabout. A rock maple was still aflame nearby, and mountain ash trees were brightly hung with orange berries.

"I would that the trees stayed red and yellow all the year through," said Marguerite, rescuing Debby from a headlong tumble on her nose.

" 'Tis a right pretty time," agreed Aunt Hepsa, taking

out her workbag. "I could do without winter myself this year."

"I don't dast to think of winter," sighed Dolly.

She was mending an old coat of Seth's, and beside her on the stone lay a pile of knitted stockings, all worn and ragged, which must be made ready for the children's feet. Marguerite took up one, turning it this way and that in her hands to see how best it might be made to do duty. She was clever at patching, but with yarn scanty and such great gaping holes it seemed a well-nigh hopeless task.

"There's but two pair o' shoes between the four young ones," Dolly was going on mournfully, "an' none for Maggie."

"Never you mind." Hepsa had her square of patch-work out now, and her needle was already moving quickly in and out of the calico scraps. "I've two pair an' she's welcome to one. I can spare them easy with my moccasins for indoors."

The children drew close to watch her fit the patch-work together, marveling at the speed of her needle and the cunning in her small, knotty fingers.

"You young ones good at answering riddles?" the old lady was asking as she worked. "You are? Well, here's one for you then. My mother used to say it to me when I was knee-high to a grasshopper." Her eyes twinkled as she repeated it, her head cocked on one side so that Marguerite thought she looked even more birdlike than usual.

> An iron horse
> With a flaxen tail;
> The faster the horse does run,
> The shorter does his tail become.

Since none of them could guess it she told them the answer with a quick wag of her head in its neat calico handkerchief.

"A needle an' thread, same's I've got here in my hand."

Even Dolly grew expansive in the older woman's cheerful company. She remembered stories out of her young days and recalled an old recipe for making cakes from cornmeal and mashed pumpkin. Marguerite listened happily as she sat sewing among the children, keeping an eye on them, particularly on the creeping Debby.

"That baby's growin' dreadful fast," observed Aunt Hepsa after Marguerite had rescued her from the end of a fallen log. "First thing you know you'll have trouble with her an' the fire. There's just one way to cure 'em of meddlin' with it. Seems pretty mean to take a hot coal to to their little fingers, but it's temptin' Providence if you don't."

"You mean burn her—on purpose?" Marguerite's eyes widened with horror.

"Yes," the other told her. "I had to do it to mine, an' Ethan too when he was little. You can't watch 'em every last minute, an' soon's your back's turned they've fallen into it or their little clothes have got afire."

Dolly snatched the baby up with one of her rare bursts of affection. "I couldn't do it," she said stoutly. "I vow I couldn't turn to an' brand no child of mine."

"Well, they're your young ones," the older woman rejoined quietly, "but I always say—better the child cry than the mother sigh."

The men were busy over the shed, Seth Jordan giving Joel a hand with the heavier logs and advice as to the door.

Caleb hung about without a look in the direction of the womenfolk. Presently they saw Ira slip away down to the shore. Soon he was pushing out in the dory with the triangle of canvas already hoisted to the pole that did duty for mast.

"Oh, look at Uncle Ira!" cried Patty.

They all followed her pointing finger with interest.

"For pity's sake, what's he up to, settin off at this time o' day?" exclaimed Dolly.

"He ain't fishin', that's sure," Aunt Hepsa remarked, shading her eyes against the sun on the water. "Looks to me like he was headin' east for the Welles place."

"He's got on his best blue coat," put in Susan.

"Then that's where he's goin' most likely."

Marguerite thought she noticed a shrewd, half-amused look pass over the old woman's face as they watched him round the eastern point.

"He might have told me," complained Dolly. "I could find work for him right here."

"Well, he's young to keep at it from sunup to sundown," the other reminded her, "an' Abby Welles is a nice girl. I'm sure I couldn't ask for no better for Ethan if he's lucky enough to get her."

It was nearly sunset when the Jordans set off for Sunday Island. Marguerite walked with Aunt Hepsa down to the strip of shingle. She held the old woman's hand, and it felt warm and light in hers, not limp and chill like so many old people's. The tide was in, filling the cove to the full. The spruces crowding the points at either side seemed to be wading in their own dark reflections.

"See how my windows shine," she pointed out to the

girl, "just like they was pure gold. It's a good thing, I always say, to see a place from other folks' land."

"They are like eyes," said Marguerite, "like two eyes looking over the water at us. I like to see them so."

Off to the northeast the line of hills showed clear and strange in reflected light. They had turned to a curious blue, deeper than Marguerite had ever seen them, as they lay heaped one upon another, faintly rugged and far.

"Isles des Monts Déserts," she murmured half to herself.

"I mean to have my new quilt just such a blue as they are now," Aunt Hepsa said, "soon's Ethan fetches me back the dye. It's only right an' proper, seein' the pattern's called 'Delectable Mountains.' "

It was well after dark when Ira beached the dory again. They could hear him whistling as he came up to the house, and he refused the mush and milk Dolly had saved for him.

"I lay the Welleses set a better table," she remarked with a sly twist to her lips as he went past her, "but like as not you wouldn't know what they put before you."

Ira shrugged, but Marguerite noticed that his eyes looked bright, and he joked with the children as he had not for some days past. Also when Dolly was putting the younger ones to bed he brought his old homespun coat to Marguerite to mend.

"Turnin' colder," he said a trifle apologetically, "an' I can't go round like a gypsy, not even in such parts."

She reached for the coat willingly. She would have liked to ask him if Abby Welles had worn the pink calico, but dared not venture so far in his confidence.

That night there was a heavy frost, and the days following were too full of work on the house and shed to allow

for more visiting. All the children even down to Jacob
were pressed into service stuffing moss between the logs,
and the sound of hammers and axes echoed from early
till late. Now flocks of wild geese flew in long wedge-
shaped companies southward. Their wings beat dark against
the blue fall skies, and no matter how they might wheel
and veer they always followed their leader out past the
islands and on tirelessly. Sometimes Joel or Ira brought
one down for their supper, but Marguerite could never
relish the taste as she did other food. It did not seem right
to kill any creature with such a compass of its own. Once
when Caleb teased her for this, Dolly unexpectedly spoke
up in her behalf.

"I don't say as Maggie's right to act so squeamish," she
had said," but I declare when I see those wild birds headin'
south so sure an' knowin' I can't help feelin' maybe they've
got more sense 'n some folks. Yes, there's plenty could take
a hint from them."

She gave a sharp look at her husband as she spoke, but
if he understood her meaning he gave no sign.

Sometimes Ira and Caleb with Pumpkin made a long
day of hunting in the woods and brought back rabbits,
fowl, and other game over their shoulders. Once they
shot a deer and dragged it back to be eaten and dried, and
the skin scraped for winter use. They reported that the
woods seemed free of Indians and that there was witchhazel growing in one spot a mile or so inland on what
appeared to be a blazed trail to the north.

"Aunt Hepsa says witchhazel works wonders for sick-
ness," Marguerite told them at supper. "I would like to
gather some for her."

"I could do with some myself," put in Dolly. "There's

nothin' like it to take down a swellin'. Do you think 'twould be safe to let Maggie an' the young ones go there alone, Ira?"

"Can't see the harm if Caleb went along with my gun," he answered, and so it was agreed upon for the day following.

Marguerite had been fearful of Caleb's making an objection at the last minute, but he liked to feel that the safety of the expedition rested upon his shoulders. Besides, he might bring down a squirrel or a rabbit to add to the store of skins he was curing to make winter caps. Pumpkin went with them, his tail bristling with excitement, his nose close to the ground as he ran before. The Flints had blazed a rough trail into the woods, but the blazes on the trees had grown faint with time and frost so that it was easy to lose the way if eyes were not sharp. Caleb knew it well, however, and kept Marguerite and the young ones firmly in tow. He carried his uncle's musket on his shoulder and allowed no loitering for the picking of late berries or bright moss.

"Supposin' we was to meet that old bear again," Patty suggested as she scampered at Marguerite's side. "What would you do without no water to douse him?"

"A bear—huh, I'd make short work o' him!" Caleb told them confidently. "An' if we followed where he was a-goin' like as not we'd find a wild honeycomb hid in some tree."

"Oh, I wouldn't mind some honey right this minute." Jacob smacked his lips at the idea.

"Well, I don't want to meet no bears or no Injuns." Susan was very firm as she picked her way between roots and bushes.

"Nor me," echoed Becky.

"Keep still then," Caleb told them shortly. "An Injun could hear you young ones gabbin' five miles away."

They kept on in silence till the witchhazel place was reached. Marguerite had never seen it growing before. The yellow fringed flowers, blooming so late, amazed her, and she liked the aromatic fragrance that came from the bark as they broke it off.

"It is like an herb Grand'mère used to keep in her cupboard," she told the children. "I did not know its name, but it had the same sharp smell."

It took longer to gather a basketful than they had expected, and Caleb grew restless. Presently he heard some squirrels chattering in nearby trees and started after them, first charging the others not to stray off in any direction.

" 'Twon't take me long, Maggie," he said. "You wait for me right here."

But the squirrels led him farther than he had thought.

"I'm tired o' this place," said Susan at last. "Let's start back along the trail."

"But we might lose our way," Marguerite reminded them. "We have not been over it so far before."

"Our eyes are just as good as Caleb's," Susan retorted, "an' I don't care if it does make him cross. He'd no call to leave us so long."

"He can catch right up with us anyway," put in Becky.

"Let us call him first," insisted Marguerite.

"Not too loud, though," reminded Susan, "account of Injuns."

They lifted up their voices, but no answer came. Marguerite felt suddenly very small and helpless there among the close-growing trees with the children about her. The sun that had made such bright patternings through the spruce boughs overhead had gone under a cloud. It was very shadowy and solemn there with the trees stretching endlessly and no shimmer of sea between the farther trunks.

"Let us go then," she heard herself saying.

In another moment they had turned about and were making for home. They kept very close to one another, and though none spoke, each knew that the other felt afraid. It was as if something they could not name kept pace with their hurrying feet. Patty stumbled on a rooty snag and fell, twisting her ankle under her and skinning her knee. She could scarcely stand on her foot again, much less walk, so Marguerite gave the basket into the twins' keeping and took the child on her back, charging Jacob to keep firm hold of her skirt lest he also fall. It was slower going after this. Marguerite's arms ached with Patty's four-year-old weight. Would they never see light between the tree trunks, she wondered?

"Seems like we'd walked for miles," Susan said presently.

"Yes," added Becky. " 'Twasn't near so long the other way, an' there ain't no sign o' that big birch with the stones piled under it."

"We must reach it soon," Marguerite assured them, but her heart sank at mention of the birch. She knew they should by now be well past it. But she must not alarm the children. She shifted Patty higher on her shoulders and tried to be cheerful. "There was a Prince in a story," she told them, "who rode into an enchanted forest and no matter how fast his horse carried him, the trees always went on ahead of him. That was how he found the Princess shut up in the tower. He had to rescue her before he could get out."

"I don't like that story," Susan spoke up, "an' I think we're lost."

Now that one of them had dared to voice the dread suspicion, they stopped in their tracks and stood facing one another in a wide-eyed little group. Patty renewed her crying from Marguerite's shoulder, and Jacob joined in from below.

"Hush!" said Marguerite, summoning all her powers. "We cannot have come far. We must find where we have stepped on the moss and twigs and follow our own steps back."

But this turned out to be more easily said than done. Their bare feet had disturbed the floor of the forest very little. Soon they were more completely astray than before. Jacob now lagged behind. It was necessary for Marguerite to set Patty down every few yards and return to fetch him in the same fashion. Sometimes they called, but though they strained their ears no answer rewarded them. Besides, they were afraid to make much noise after Caleb's warning about Indians.

"If only Pumpkin would hear us and come," sighed Marguerite, "we could follow him back. He has such a good nose for scents, surely he will come soon." But though she cheered them on, her own spirits grew heavier each moment. She remembered what Ira had said about the Indian trail going north. She could not help wondering whether they had chanced upon it. Perhaps they were even then walking into the Indian country, to be tomahawked or carried far, far off as other settlers' families had been before them. "Mon Dieu," she prayed under her breath, "help us to find the way home!"

And then, as they floundered on through the underbrush with rain beginning to fall, they all stopped short before a solid wall of rock that reached many feet above their heads. Ferns and low-growing trees covered it, and they were turning back in discouragement when Marguerite's quick eyes spied a narrow opening in the rock.

"It is a cave," she said. "Perhaps we can rest there till the rain is over."

"It's dreadful dark inside," said Becky, hanging back.

"Maybe there's bears," Susan suggested.

"I will go in first," Marguerite told them, setting Patty down and pushing aside the vines that half-obscured the opening. "Wait here till I call you."

With beating heart she stepped in, taking care to keep close to the wall of rock. At first she could see nothing; then as her eyes became used to the dimness she made out a lighter place, nearer the center of the cave. Evidently there was an opening above, like a rough chimney, down which a pale shaft of light came. Even as she noticed this she became aware of a peculiar smell, unlike any she had ever known. There was dankness in the cave and the walls dripped, but the smell was something other than this. She could not have said why, but more than the darkness or the bats that swooped unpleasantly near her head, this smell terrified her. She shivered, but she must go on. A weasel scuttled away at her approach, and a scattered pebble clinked with a hollow sound. It was only a few feet to the opening under the light, but it took all her courage to force herself there.

"I do not like this place," she panted; "it is evil."

She could see now that the hole above her head was round and blackened as if by smoke from many fires. The light came wanly through and the green of spruces showed in the opening. A great flat stone resting on two round ones was directly below, and in the queer half-light it seemed to the girl's excited fancy that she could make out queer cuttings on it, rough letters and pictures chiseled in the stone. Below it were the remains of a fire, charred logs, broken clay dishes, and some scattered white fragments that turned her suddenly cold all over. She stood there under the greenish light with both hands pressed against her beating heart, trying to tell herself that it was nothing—this burnt-out fire, this pile of bones, and a queer smell she had not smelled before. But she knew better.

She began to tremble, and the smell sickened her through and through. Something glittered at her feet. She forced herself to stoop and pick it up. It was a tarnished buckle, such as might fasten a child's shoe, and nearby was a lock of hair—a long fine strand of reddish yellow, but dark and stiffened at the roots.

"Oh, mon Dieu," she whispered, and she felt her own fingers shakily making the sign of the cross.

She had not even breath enough to cry out as she thrust it into her pocket along with the buckle and stumbled out into the woods once more. The children were as she had left them by the opening. She caught up Patty with such suddenness that the child cried out, and the twins and Jacob ran after her in a panic. She took no heed of how they went crashing through the underbush. All that mattered was to be well away from that place.

"You're white's a sheet, Maggie!" Susan cried when they stopped at last to catch their breath.

"An' I never see your eyes so big!" Becky told her. "What was in that there cave?"

"You must not ask me—not ever." Marguerite's lips trembled, and she gave a startled look behind her. "Come." And she urged them on again in the opposite direction.

She could feel her pocket sagging heavily at every step, and it seemed to her that nothing had ever sounded so good to her ears as Pumpkin's distant barking.

He came bounding toward them, his whole yellow body wriggling with joy at the reunion.

"Good dog! Good fellow!" cried the twins, flinging themselves upon him.

"Chien, mon brave chien," echoed Marguerite.

They gave themselves utterly into his charge, following his pointing nose back to the trail and their own clearing. But before they reached it a very frightened Caleb appeared. His relief at seeing them was so great that he immediately lost his temper.

"You're a fine lot!" he told them with a ferocious scowl. "I can't turn my back without you get yourselves lost an' have me chasin' these woods for miles."

"You should not go off to hunt squirrels!" Marguerite retorted, her heart still pounding at the memory of all they had been through. "You were sent to watch out for us."

"An' you should have done as I said," he insisted. "I always heard you couldn't trust a Frenchman, an' it's the same way with you, I guess."

"You leave Maggie alone, Caleb Sargent!" cried the twins hotly. "She's got more sense'n you have."

"She's nothin' but a Bound-out Girl," he blazed, his face growing dark with anger under his sunburn and freckles, "an' I'll show her who's givin' orders round here."

He turned on his heel and marched ahead, his shoulders very stiff under the musket and the dead squirrels strung on a thong. In this fashion they returned to the log house with the sun going down behind the western islands.

"Wherever have you young ones been?" cried Dolly Sargent from the doorway. "I've been near distracted watchin' for you."

"You better ask Maggie," Caleb answered in aggrieved tones. "I'm 'most done for thrashin' the woods after 'em."

"We got lost," Susan explained, "when he went off to hunt squirrels."

"Yes," put in Becky, "an' it's a wonder we didn't meet with bears or Injuns back there in the big woods."

Marguerite set Patty on the doorstep and sank down beside her. She felt too spent for words just then. The cave and its ugly secret were still too near to her. She let Caleb bluster and the children wrangle without interference while she washed and bound Patty's hurts.

She scarcely heard the scoldings that came her way as they gathered round the table for supper, and it was only after the younger children were asleep under the quilts that she broke her silence. The two men and Caleb were busy whittling some wooden spoons before the fire, and Dolly sat nearby with her knitting. In the light of the blazing spruce logs Marguerite told them of the cave.

"I knew it was an evil place," she wound up. "I knew it even before I came to the stone under the hole and found the old fire and those bones." She shivered at the memory, and her eyes grew enormous.

"What's there to that?" Caleb broke in scornfully. "Somebody made a fire an' roasted a deer in there, most likely."

"Hush, Caleb!" ordered his father, the knife and the piece of wood idle in his hands. "Go on, Maggie. What made you think 'twas a bad place?"

"It was that terrible smell," she told him, "and those marks on the stone, like—like evil signs, and then—these." She pulled the lock of hair and the buckle from her pocket and laid them on his knee.

None of them spoke for a full minute. It was so still in the room that the snapping of the fire and the sea shuffling the pebbles down in the cove seemed strangely loud. The buckle shone faintly in the firelight, and when Joel laid down his knife and took up the strand of hair it showed bright between his fingers.

"A scalp lock." Caleb was the first to break silence. "See the skin stickin' to it."

"An' it never belonged to no Injun," Ira said slowly.

"It's a woman's, or a child's—" Dolly had gone suddenly white to the lips.

"Weren't there no others?" Caleb was asking.

"I do not know," Marguerite answered. "I ran without once looking back."

"Just like a girl to do that," complained Caleb. "Soon's ever they get a chance at anythin' they run away."

"Be quiet!" Joel Sargent spoke sternly. "This is a grave matter."

"You remember what Jordan told us that first day we landed," Ira reminded them; "how he said the Injuns held this place was theirs 'count o' their spirits or some such notion."

"Yes," said Dolly. "I recall he did say so when they wanted we should build elsewhere."

"Well, I think maybe it's somewhat to do with this cave Maggie got into," Ira went on thoughtfully. "Every spring he 'lowed there's queer doin's hereabouts. I wouldn't wonder if that's where they kill or torture their captives."

"I've heard tell o' such doin's," Joel answered gravely. "At any rate these belonged to white folks." He put the hair and buckle into an inner pocket of his shirt before he spoke again. "There's to be no talk o' this to the neighbors, mind you."

"But maybe they'd know who it belonged to," began Caleb.

"You're not to say so much as a word of it," his father told him, "not you nor Maggie. There's been trouble enough about settlin' this point without we have 'em turn agin us."

"An' just when they're commencin' to act so friendly an' all," put in Dolly quickly.

"Remember now, Maggie," Joel Sargent charged her, "an' tomorrow you'll go along with Ira an' me to see if we can find that place again."

After that they banked the fire and turned in for the night. But Marguerite could hear the sound of low voices long after she had crawled in beside the sleeping twins. She knew that Joel and Dolly were discussing it together in the next room, and she lay wide-eyed for a long time because no sooner did she close her eyes than the cave and all that she had seen there returned to her all too plainly. She could not help feeling grateful that rain fell in torrents the next day and the one following.

But though she and the men went on two searching expeditions, they never came upon the cave or its cleverly hidden entrance. Pumpkin might have guided them to it but for the rains washing away their scent, and Marguerite could not find it in her heart to be regretful.

One day a week or so later Seth Jordan appeared with an invitation from Aunt Hepsa.

"She means to set up the loom for weavin'," he explained, "an' she wants you should let Maggie an' the twins come to help. They can stay the night an' I'll fetch 'em back. She's lonesome with Ethan gone."

Marguerite scarcely dared lift her eyes from her work till Dolly's consent was given. She wanted to sing and shout with the twins, who ran before her down to the cove.

"Mind you an' the twins behave yourselves. Don't make no trouble," Dolly Sargent called after her from the doorstep, where she stood with Debby in her arms and Jacob and Patty at her skirts.

"Yes'm," Marguerite answered dutifully enough for all that her spirits ran high with anticipation.

"Good-by, Maggie!" called Jacob and Patty after her, their voices shrill on the morning air. "Good-by!"

Aunt Hepsa lost no time in putting them all to work. The weaving shed was already full of wool, dye pots, and mysterious pieces of wood.

"I've been spinnin' like one possessed these days," she told her guests cheerfully. "Now I've got all the longest thread ready. You two little girls can sit over there on the floor an' wind those short lengths onto corncobs same's I've commenced doin'. I'll need Maggie to set up the loom."

"My, but it is big," said Marguerite, regarding the great wooden frame with awe.

" 'Tis so," agreed Aunt Hepsa, "but my mother always used to say 'the heavier the loom, the lighter for the weaver,' an' I've always found it that way."

Now she was showing the girl how to go about the "beaming" or "drawing through." This was a long and difficult piece of work, requiring more than one pair of hands to pass the thread through the teeth of the long wooden "rake" that ran across the middle beam. Each thread must be drawn separately through an opening which the old lady called "the harness eye," and must be set according to the draft or pattern. Marguerite could make nothing of this. It seemed to be a series of strange dots and dashes in faded pen strokes on a sheet of worn, brown paper.

"It looks like magic," she told her hostess seriously.

"Well, it ain't," smiled the other. "Every one of these here marks is as plain to me as the foreign gibberish you know how to talk."

Marguerite turned to with a will. She had taken her place on a low bench in front of the loom where she could receive the thread ends as they came through the harness eyes. At first she was clumsy at the handling; her thumbs got in the way, and she dropped or confused the threads. But soon she grew more skillful. Her brown fingers moved surely and steadily. She hardly ever missed the strands as the other passed them through to her.

"This here's goin' to be 'Whig Rose' pattern," Hepsa explained, "for a good warm winter spread. That reddish wool I dyed from sassafras bark will go good with the bay-leaf yellow."

"But how do you make the pattern, Aunt Hepsa?" The twins left their winding to draw near.

"You'll see when the time comes," she told them. "I do it with my foot on this treadle. That raises or lowers the warp threads—so."

"You 'n me, we make a good team," she said during a pause as she bent to splice two ends of thread. "I expect we could weave an' spin our fingers to the bone without ever tirin'."

"I do expect so," Marguerite acquiesced with a little sigh, "if it was not that I am a Bound-out Girl."

"You won't be one always," Aunt Hepsa told her comfortingly. "You'll be marryin' with a home of your own before long."

"I belong to the Sargents for six years yet," she reminded the other. "Many things can happen in six years."

"There's no denyin' that, but when you're as old as I be, you get to take whatever comes along." She fastened the threads before she went on in a different tone. "But one thing's certain—you need a pair o' shoes, an' I mean to see you have 'em."

That was a day to remember, with the sweet smells, the good food, the wonder of seeing the colored strands of wool turning into patterns of firm, warm cloth under Aunt Hepsa's hands, the setting up of the smaller loom to make linsey-woolsey cloth for them all. This was a simpler matter, involving no special pattern, for the wool would be woven on linen warp in its natural state with only a darker thread at intervals to give it a grayish color. Marguerite caught the manner of this quickly. As long as the light lasted she kept the shuttle flying back and forth. The clack of the wood beat out a sure and steady rhythm, of which she seemed herself a part.

Supper was plentiful; the Sargents had not known plenty since the Raising. The twins' eyes grew round at the sight of frying eggs, besides the fresh corn cakes and bowls of milk. Marguerite ate with relish. It seemed most wonderfully pleasant to her to be at a quiet table set with proper plates and mugs; to handle pewter spoons once more. After the meal was over Seth brought out his fiddle and played a tune or two for Susan and Becky while Marguerite helped Aunt Hepsa with the dishes.

When the little girls were in bed, the old woman got Seth to bring out a piece of cowhide and draw the pattern of Marguerite's feet on it. Then she showed her how to pull the leather up over the toes and instep, till it fitted snug and firm with thongs to keep it in place.

"They make easy steppin'," Aunt Hepsa told her; "an' likely you'll need to wear 'em inside the boots I promised you, your foot's that much narrower."

Seth took an old lantern and went out to see to the cows. He returned presently, calling them to join him at the door.

"Northern Lights," he was saying, "the like I've never seen before."

Marguerite followed his pointing finger, and sure enough the northern sky was bristling with strange lights. Long fingers of ghostly white pulsated almost to the mid-heavens from above the dark line of shore across the channel. Sometimes wheels of ice-green color moved through them, and again flashes of red fire appeared and disappeared eerily. Always in utter silence they flared or burned, a stillness that sent queer chills down the backbone.

"That double ring o' brightness is the Aurora Borealis," Seth told them. "It don't often show up so clear."

"But what does it mean?" asked Marguerite, her heart strangely shaken at the sight.

"Cold weather mostly," he told her, "unless you believe same's the Injun's do that it's a sign o' war an' famine."

"You'd ought to be ashamed o' yourself to talk such a way to the girl, Seth," his aunt scolded him as she stepped briskly inside and pulled the door to on the spectacle. "All I know is it means winter's here an' no mistake. An' I'd know that by the feelin' in my bones without no Northern Lights to tell me."

PART 3   WINTER

Ethan and Timothy had been back some days now, and their boat unloaded of its goods. There was to be a corn-shelling bee at Sunday Island that very day, which put all the Sargent family in high good humor except Ira. He had been moody and low-spirited ever since the sloop's return, and Marguerite suspected this might in some way be connected with the six china teacups it was rumored that Ethan had brought back for Abby Welles. No one had set eyes on them as yet, but Timothy had told Dolly Sargent that they were sprigged and had cost Ethan a pretty penny.

"Near a pound sterling," Dolly had enlarged upon the story, "or I miss my guess. I know the price real china teacups bring in Boston, an' it stands to reason they'd be dearer in Portsmouth."

"Ethan must be mighty taken with Abby Welles to squander a pound sterling on her," Joel had observed with a sidelong glance at his brother. "But I hear he drove a good bargain over his dried fish an' furs."

"He's good at drivin' bargains, Ethan is," was all Ira had said, but Marguerite noticed that his forehead was drawn into troubled lines.

It was raw November weather now, and an ugly sea

was running in the channel. Joel and Caleb rowed the big
dory, with Dolly, the twins, and Debby for ballast; while
Ira took Marguerite and the two younger children in the
skiff. It was hard work pulling against the chop. In spite
of Ira's skill with the oars, icy spray and salt water splashed
them often, and Jacob and Patty huddled closer under the
old shawl. Marguerite wore the cowhide slippers and
stockings Aunt Hepsa had given her, but her dress of
brown homespun was old and patched. Dolly had fitted
her out in it when she had first been bound-out to them,
and now after the summer's activity, the girl had well-
nigh outgrown it. The skirt that should have reached
her ankles was halfway up to her knees, and the waist
fitted so snugly that Dolly had shaken her head, declar-
ing it hardly decent. Over this she wore an old cloak and
hood of Dolly's, as much too big for her as the dress was
too small. But she was too happy in the prospect of the
shelling bee to let this disturb her, and at least she knew
that her dark braids were smooth and freshly tied with
snippets of yellow wool.

"There'll be molasses cakes," Patty was saying for the
tenth time. "Aunt Hepsa told me so."

"For all of us," put in Jacob solemnly, "but only if we
shell lots of ears."

Ira did not laugh and tease the children as he would
have done earlier in the summer. Marguerite glanced at
him quickly and saw that his lips were set close, and
though his eyes took note of shore and waves, they seemed
turned upon some inner matter within himself. The wind
blew his thick, reddish-brown hair over his forehead, and
she saw that he had shaved away the stubble from his

chin. If only she had had her rosary she would have said a prayer or two in secret for Ira, that he might grow merry again, and if Abby Welles be the desire of his heart, that she might prefer him to Ethan Jordan. But of these thoughts she made no mention. She had no rosary now, and besides, she felt that the feelings of another were not a fit subject for idle prattle.

It was almost as great an occasion as the Raising and far less hard work for the men. The Jordan kitchen and the shed beyond it were filled with heaps of dried ears of corn, from which the earlier arrivals were already shredding the yellow kernels into troughs made from hollowed logs. As usual Marguerite was put in charge of the younger children.

"They're too little to handle even real dull knives," Aunt Hepsa had decided, "so you help 'em pile up the cobs by this door, Maggie."

All the neighbors were there now, except the Morses, whose baby was ailing. Marguerite could see Abby Welles moving from kitchen to pantry and back again as she helped Aunt Hepsa set out the food. She wore a dress of blue linsey with a white kerchief crossed in front. Her cheeks were deeply pink from the heat of the fire, and she was, as Aunt Hepsa said, "pretty as a posy." There was great talking and laughter about a red ear of corn. Marguerite could not make it all out, but it appeared that whoever found this would be lucky in love and marry before the year was out.

"Ethan he must be sot on gettin' it," chuckled Caleb to Marguerite, in an unusually expansive mood as he passed. "I s'pose if he shells the most ears he reckons he can't miss it."

But it was not to Ethan or Abby Welles that the ear fell. Marguerite never knew what made her peer into the corner behind the wooden trough now already filled, but when she did, there it was—the coveted red ear.

"It must have rolled there," she thought, her heart beating fast with excitement at such a discovery, "but I found it all the same!"

No one was looking in her direction. Even the children had gathered round the shellers by the other trough. She reached down and pulled it out quickly, hiding it under a fold of her dress.

"By Godfrey, it's got to turn up soon!" she heard Ethan exclaim, his hands making the yellow kernels fly from the cobs.

"It's mine! I've got the red ear!" The words were on the tip of her tongue, but somehow she did not say them.

An idea had come into her head, and now it was there, she could not forget it. Searching the group beyond her, she could see Ira standing a little gloomy and apart. He also shelled the corn, but not as Ethan was doing, and Abby's eyes were not upon him at the moment. Still keeping her treasure out of sight, Marguerite slipped over to stand beside him.

"Ira," she said, but the noise of the others drowned her voice. He looked straight before him at the bent heads and moving fingers. It was only when she pressed closer and plucked at his sleeve that he noticed her.

"What you want?" he asked her absently, his eyes still watching the others.

"Here," she whispered to him, under cover of the laughter about the trough. "You take it."

Another second and the coveted red ear of corn was

in his hands, while she was slipping away with one thin brown forefinger at her lips in sign of warning. No one had noticed what passed between them or seen the sudden smile of understanding he flashed to her across the shed before he held the treasure out for all the rest to see.

"Uncle Ira's got it!" shouted the twins, jumping up and down excitedly, their stiff braids bobbing on their shoulders. "He's got the red ear!"

"Well, he's a sly one, he is," Seth Jordan spoke up, "lettin' us all shell our fingers off an' him standin' there with it all the time!"

Marguerite's cheeks grew hot under her tan, hearing the laughter and joking, knowing so well how he had come by it.

"You better watch out for him, Abby," her brother Timothy was teasing, "an' you too, Ethan."

They kept it up a long time after they had finished the shelling and were gathered about the long table in the kitchen. From her place at the far end among the children Marguerite heard and rejoiced to see Ira so merry and smiling again. After all, she thought, six sprigged china teacups were not everything. She felt sorry she had not been able to set a better patch in Ira's jacket. She had done her best, but it showed as queer and crooked as the one on the sail of the *Isabella B.*

Before they began to eat Seth Jordan bowed his head and they all did likewise, even to Jacob and Patty.

"O Lord," he said solemnly, "bless our crops an' our cattle an' all here gathered—"

He paused, uncertain of the words that should follow, but another voice—a woman's—spoke up from across the table.

"An' keep us safe from Injun raids. *Amen*," it added.

"*Amen*." They all joined in, and Marguerite made a quick sign of the cross, which it was as well no one saw.

The feast was more plentiful and varied than any Marguerite had tasted since she had left France, but it was what followed the meal that stayed longest in her memory; for when the table was cleared and the dishes washed and put away, Seth brought out his fiddle and played all the tunes he knew over and over again. Ethan had fetched him back new fiddle strings, and the bow scraped them swiftly and well. It was wonderful, Marguerite thought, to see how Seth's knotty brown fingers moved up and down, picking the notes out and sending them to fill the kitchen with delightsome sound. Sometimes the higher ones squeaked and broke off, but no one minded, and he never lagged in his time, so that feet were continually beating an accompanying rhythm on the broad floorboards. Sometimes he played tunes they all knew, and then the room was filled full of voices; sometimes only Aunt Hepsa's would be lifted up in her sweet, thin old piping. She sang the ballad of "Springfield Mountain," a sad tale of a young lover who died of a snake's bite, and to Marguerite's joy, she was prevailed upon to sing all the verses of "Calico Bush." Even though it was already familiar to the girl, she found herself quickening to the recital of the young man's suffering at the hands of his proud love Judy.

> The snow it fell and the winds did blow
> I wandered high and I wandered low
> Till night came on me black as a crow,
> And never a light did shine or show,
> *Calico, sprigged calico!*

The final warning had never seemed more sad and solemn.

> So, maids who pass where the laurels grow,
> Think on this tale of long ago.
> Set not your hearts on a furbelow,
> Lest you live to curse sprigged calico,
>   *Calico, sprigged calico!*

And then the chairs and benches were pushed back and Seth was playing a reel.

"Ils vont danser!" Marguerite could scarcely believe her eyes, but it was so. The women were lining themselves on one side and the men and boys on the other. She felt herself between the twins, who were tugging excitedly at her hands. It was not like any of the dances she had danced in France, but more of a game or round, with each man in turn joining hands with his opposite partner and swinging her round while the others clapped and sang in chorus:

> Here's the couple that stole the sheep,
> While all the rest were fast asleep.
> Put the salt right in the hand,
> And call "Here Nanny, Nanny, Nan!"

Round and round they twirled, two by two, with the hands clapping and the voices shouting in hearty singsong:

> Oars in the boat and they won't go round,
> Oars in the boat and they won't go round
> Till you've kissed the pretty girl you've just found.

Such laughter and smacking up and down the line! Marguerite felt her blood tingling and her heart thumping pleasantly even though Caleb was her opposite partner and his twirlings were anything but graceful.

When it was over everyone stopped, flushed and panting, except Ira, who continued to twirl Abby for some time after the music stopped.

"Come on, Aunt Hepsa, do us a jog!" someone begged, and Seth struck into another quick tune.

Although she protested, the old woman was nothing loath to show that she had a light foot. She stepped out gayly and alone to the middle of the kitchen floor and began to spin till her skirts stood out stiffly about her in the wind she made. Her feet in their homemade slippers went through the quick steps deftly—heel and toe, dip and spin, left foot, right foot, in and out. Marguerite watched in delighted wonder, seeing the old figure move so surely, watching the pink come into her cheeks till they were bright as the children's.

"Whew!" she panted at last, sinking down breathless on the settle and flapping her apron to fan her flushed face. "I ain't made such a fool o' myself in months. But anyhow my knees ain't so stiff's I thought."

"Who'll be next?" Seth was asking, tightening his fiddle strings in readiness.

"I will," Marguerite heard herself saying, "I will dance the pavane."

She saw the astonished looks on the children's faces and the disapproval on Dolly's and Hannah Welles' as she stepped into the cleared place in the middle. But Aunt Hepsa gave her an encouraging nod, and Seth swung into the reel again.

"Allons!" she said to herself, and her feet began to move in the steps she had not thought of for so long.

It was not the same tune that Oncle Pierre had played when he had taught her, but it would do. She could point her toes and slide as well to this one. Her body could dip and bend as easily here in the Jordans' kitchen to Seth's fiddle as it had across the sea in Le Havre. All the motions of the dance came back to her like the notes of a remembered tune. She was free again and so light she scarcely felt the floor under her feet. Now she was whirling so swiftly that the faces of the little group about her were nothing but a pale blur. One of her braids shook loose. She felt the hair warm and tumbling about her cheek and shoulders; and the ring and button, swinging on the cord inside her dress, thumped at every move. Only when the music stopped abruptly did she pause. Even then it was a full moment before she came to her proper senses.

Tongues were clicking all about her.

"I declare, child, you're the smartest stepper I ever see!" Hepsa Jordan exclaimed. "I wouldn't think a skinny little body like you could keep it up so!"

"It's a caution to see her," one of the men spoke up.

"Yes," agreed another, "I've heard tell the French was light steppers!"

"An' light-minded and light-fingered as well." Marguerite heard Joel Sargent's voice, heavy with disapproval.

"I wasn't brought up to such doin's," Hannah Welles broke in, "and if any child of mine had stepped about so I'd be pure shamed, that's what I'd be."

"She's raised different, bein' French," Marguerite could hear Dolly apologizing. "She don't mean no harm, but it's in her blood, I guess."

"Oh, come now, where's the hurt?" protested Seth, laying away his fiddle. "I thought she jigged it right an' proper."

"*Proper* ain't hardly the word for it," put in Kate Stanley from her corner. "An' if she was bound-out to me—"

"It says in my Bible as how King David danced before the Lord, an' it don't appear that He made any objections," Hepsa Jordan remarked with a finality that put an end to the argument.

Marguerite listened to their words, her heart still pounding under her homespun waist, the blood still tingling in her veins from such joyous exertions. Now she felt suddenly tired and low-spirited. It had seemed so natural and easy and right to dance to Seth's fiddle. Why must they think ill of her for it? She turned toward the window, pressing her cheeks to the little glass panes to cool them of their smarting.

It was as she did so that she saw the thin column of smoke across the channel, a faint blue spiral rising from the woods behind the Sargent point. The early winter afternoon was slipping into night, but there was still light enough for her to be sure, and the sight filled her with dread. The remembrance of the cave was upon her. She felt sickened at the memory, and the smoke still rose in a warning thread over the tops of the pointed trees. Behind her in the kitchen the dull booming of their talk seemed as far removed from her as the sea breaking on the outer ledges. She knew she must summon words to tell them, and at the same time she knew she must take care; she recalled Joel's warning the night she had shown him the lock of hair and the buckle— "There's to be no talk of this, mind you."

Caleb passed her and she pulled at his hand.

"Regardez-là," she whispered. "I mean—look over there."

As he followed her pointing finger his blue eyes narrowed, and the jeering smile with which he always greeted any lapse into French died on his lips.

"Injuns!" he said under his breath. "Must be."

He hurried over to his father, and after that there was a babble of voices out of which Marguerite made little but that the smoke across the water had laid a chill on everyone in the warm kitchen. They all agreed it could have but one meaning.

"We've been free of Injuns too long," Hannah Welles spoke up. "I thanked God every night for it. But now we'll live in dread of our lives again." Her face looked drawn and troubled.

"It may be but a small party on their way north," Stanley suggested hopefully.

"Not likely," said Seth, who had already got down his gun and powder horn from the chimney. "That's a big fire to send up a smoke like that. Comes from the same place where there was trouble last spring after Flint went. I told you to leave that land alone, Sargent. They'll drive you out sooner or later."

"Not me, they won't." Joel Sargent had already slung his musket over his shoulder.

"Well, the house is standin' yet," Aunt Hepsa reminded them as she peered against the gathering twilight.

"I'd be obliged if you'd keep Dolly an' the young ones here tonight," Marguerite heard Sargent say to her. "Ira an' Caleb an' I'll go over now."

"Oh, no, Joel, don't you go," Dolly was begging. "There's maybe a hundred of 'em, and what'll you three be against that?"

"But I can't stay here an' let 'em burn our house to the ground same's they did before," he told her. "After the work it was to raise it I aim to keep it if I can."

The men drew apart in a little group, hurriedly discussing the best means of defense. They all had their muskets in hand, and Ethan was filling his powder horn while they talked. Although they disapproved of Sargent's settling where he had they were not neighbors to refuse help. So it was finally decided that Ethan and Timothy Welles should join the three in the defense of the log house.

"That'll leave Stanley an' Nathan Welles to help me keep guard here," Seth explained. "I doubt their places an' the Morses' are in danger. Chances are the Injuns will move north when they go, not east nor westward."

Patty and the twins and Kate Stanley were crying with fright in a little group about Marguerite's skirts, and Jacob's eyes filled with tears as he listened.

"I'm afeard for Pumpkin, Maggie," he whispered, pressing close to her. "I don't want no Injun to get him."

"I guess he can run faster than they can." Marguerite tried to reassure him, but her heart smote her remembering how the dog had begged to come.

The women and children clustered round the door to see them go. Seth and the other men went with them down to the water to help push the boats off. Joel and Caleb and Ethan Jordan were already lost to sight behind the wooded patch between house and shore, and Timothy Welles and Ira were moving after them in the dwindling half-light when Marguerite saw Abby Welles break away from the little group.

"Ira," she heard her call in a voice so sharp with entreaty

that it no longer seemed to belong to the quiet, soft-eyed girl in the blue linsey dress. "Ira, don't you go over there. Don't you do it."

"Why, Abby—" Marguerite heard him plainly though she could not see either of their faces. "I've got to go. You mustn't take on so."

"But if—if anything happened to you. . . . If the Injuns—" Abby had reached his side, and Marguerite felt her own cheeks growing hot to see, even in the dimness, how he set down his musket to draw her close with his free arm. "Oh, please make one of the other men go in your place."

His answer was too low for Marguerite to catch, but for a moment she saw them cling together before he moved after Timothy into the wood path. There was a queer silence when Abby rejoined the women, and Marguerite thought she heard her crying as she went past.

"So that's the way the wind blows, is it?" she heard Hannah Welles saying to her daughter from the doorstep.

"Leave her be, Hannah," Hepsa Jordan put in. "A girl don't know her own heart till she's had a smell o' danger."

"She shouldn't have took Ethan's teacups," the other reminded her.

"Maybe not," observed Hepsa, "but I tell you love's got nothin' to do with chinaware, if my own flesh an' blood did fetch 'em back to her."

But there was no more talk of love that night under the Jordan roof. Darkness was on them even before the three men and young Andrew Stanley came up from the shore. They kept watch by turns at the two seaward-facing windows, straining their eyes against the darkness for any sudden flare. That was to be the signal in case of need, for to fire a musket would be foolhardy and a waste of precious gunpowder as well.

"They'll keep to the house till morning," Seth said. "I told 'em not to risk unbankin' the fires. Those Injuns have got noses a mile long."

"Queer we don't hear that dog o' theirs bark," remarked Aunt Hepsa. "Some nights when it's still like this I can hear him real plain across the channel, an' he'd likely make a rumpus when they landed."

Jacob and Patty began to cry again at this, and though Marguerite did her best to comfort them, she also felt grave misgivings. She would have preferred to stay in the kitchen with the men and older women, but the children must be kept from under foot and she climbed with them into the loft where Ethan and Seth usually slept. It was shadowy up there, but snug under the low rafters. Aunt Hepsa had given them some old quilts to spread on the floor since the two beds would not hold them all. The twins and Kate Stanley whispered together for a long time, but at last their breathing grew quiet and they slept. William Stanley and Jacob were also asleep in the other bed, and Patty, curled up in a quilt beside her on the floor, had finally stopped her low whimpering.

But Marguerite could not do likewise. Every nerve in her body was alert, taut as the strings on Seth Jordan's fiddle. She tried to close her eyes, but that was no use. She must open them again to see the chinks of light coming between knotholes and cracks in the floorboards. Her ears, too, were strained to hear any words of the low-voiced talk going on in the room below. Once she heard Debby give a low wail and Aunt Hepsa go into the pantry to fetch her a drink of milk. Sometimes the muskets thumped on wooden boards as the men changed places at the windows. Sometimes she heard another log being thrown on the fire and a quick sizzling as the flames caught at the bark. Once she recognized Abby Welles' voice in the talk below, and she wondered what she had said and what she must be feeling. She found herself thinking of Ira and the red ear of corn, though that seemed to have happened years ago, as if it were part of Le Havre or the days before they left Marblehead. Of course, she told herself, it couldn't really mean all that they had said. Abby must have loved Ira before she, Marguerite, had slipped it into his hand, yet it had all turned out so queerly, just like a book or an old ballad. Maybe there would be a song about it sometime, even as there was about the Calico Bush; and people would sing it long after they were all dead and gone. But romances and ballads were apt to be sad at the end. It mustn't be like that for Ira and Abby Welles. Le Bon Dieu must have it explained to Him how important it was that the Indians should stay away from their house. It meant so much to them all as well as to Ira and Abby. Surely if He knew about those logs and how hard it had been to cut and drag and set them in place, He would not be so cruel as to let harm come to them. She began to pray desperately there in the darkness, a queer mixture of Latin and French and such English as she could muster.

"O, Pater Noster, Ave Maria, Regina Coelorum," she prayed, "let not the savages do us harm! Bon Dieu et les Saints en gloire, send them away from these parts before there is bloodshed, je Te prie. Spare all our lives, and the house too, please. Domine, ad adjuvandum me festina. O, Lord, make haste to help me!"

Over and over she repeated it, counting it on her fingers as she had her old rosary prayers. Ten times, twenty times, thirty times, forty times, and then fifty. Soon it would reach a hundred and that could not fail to help.

She awoke to sunlight slanting through a small window shaped like an eyebrow under the eaves. So it was morning again. She had fallen asleep in the midst of her prayers, and the children still slept in heaps about her under Aunt Hepsa's quilts. She could hear the fire snapping below and someone stepping about the kitchen. Softly she slid out of the quilt folds so as not to rouse the children, and down the steep, ladder-like stairs. Aunt Hepsa was moving about the kitchen, and Abby Welles stood at the table setting out dishes. She gave Marguerite a rather wan smile, and her eyes looked as if she had not slept all through the night. There were no signs of the men and their muskets. Aunt Hepsa explained in a whisper that they had already eaten and were setting out for the point. The log house was still standing, Marguerite could see that in the early morning light. Their eyes met in relief over this.

"Let 'em sleep a spell longer," the old woman whispered, nodding in the direction of the bedroom. "They didn't have a wink till the sun came up, and heaven only knows what kind of a day we may be in for."

But it turned out not so disastrous as they had feared. The party returning to the house the night before had been unmolested. The chief loss, it developed, was old Brindle and her calf. They had been taken from the shed along with a bag of meal. Evidently Pumpkin had defended the place to the best of his powers. There were paw marks in the soft earth thereabouts, and, alas, traces of blood farther up the trail. Judging by the smell of the smoke in the woods there had been roast meat—little chance that they would ever see the poor animals again. What troubled them all now was fear of another sally from the woods.

"They'll be just fit for a fight with all that fresh meat inside 'em," Seth said. "You'd best leave the women an' young ones on the Island a spell."

But Joel Sargent was against this. He sensed his neighbors' disapproval, and he was not one to ask favors. They did not say so much to his face, but he guessed what they were thinking and that they blamed him bitterly behind his back.

"We'll make out," he told them the next noon when they had all landed on the point, even Marguerite and the younger children in the last boatload from Sunday Island. "The baby's old enough to live without cow's milk, an' between us Ira an' me can hold off quite a pack of Injuns."

"If we hear firing we'll come straight across to you," Seth promised.

"Looks like a storm anyhow," Timothy Welles added, squinting off to the Mount Desert hills, which barely showed in a grayish blur, "an' that means they'd keep under cover till it's past."

"It's my opinion this wasn't any regular band of the Tarratines," Nathan Welles added. "More likely some three or four on their way north, run out o' food an' helped themselves to yours."

"All the same," put in Dolly Sargent, "we'll keep well indoors till the danger's over. Better lose the cows 'n any of our scalps."

Timothy Welles was right about the storm. Clouds were

piling up to the east and north, and the sea was growing rough. No time to waste in talk if the men were to get home before it set in. So off they went in different directions, their boats dwindling to specks on the heaving slate-gray water.

"I declare I can't bring myself to watch 'em out of sight," said Dolly, turning into the house. "Who knows what may happen afore they come again?"

By late afternoon the storm had settled into a steady northeast blow with rain driving furiously against the log house, pouring in miniature cascades off the roof. They had closed the outer wooden shutters against it, so what light there was came from the fire. In spite of four great logs and the handfuls of cones they added from time to time, it burned badly. Rain pelted down the chimney, sending smoke into the room and making fitful splutterings.

"Smoke's in my eyes," complained Patty, rubbing them with her fists till they were red. "It smarts!"

"Yours ain't the only ones that do," Caleb told her crossly. "I can't hardly see to whittle this spoon I'm makin', they keep waterin' so."

"It is well the good Sisters taught me to knit without looking at my needles," Marguerite told the children, her fingers busy with the wool, "for I should certainly drop many stitches because of these tears."

"You're lucky if you don't shed no worse ones," came from Dolly as she rocked Debby in the old cradle.

Ira paid little heed to them. He seemed busy with his own thoughts, which Marguerite guessed had much to do with Abby Welles and all that had taken place at the corn-shelling. Joel sat moodily hollowing part of a spruce trunk to make a water barrel. He looked tired from anxiety and lack of sleep. He had grown a rough, grayish brown beard that summer, which made him look years older, so Marguerite thought, than when they had all set off from Marblehead.

"We've got but four o' the sixteen hens we fetched with us," he was saying to his wife. "Three we lost to other wild birds, an' the Injuns must have helped themselves to the rest. It's a wonder these escaped."

"There'll be precious few eggs this winter," she sighed, "an' what with Brindle an' the calf gone I don't see how we're to make out."

"You'll never starve so near the sea," he reminded her. "It's never so bad but what we can get fish an' birds."

They talked but little as they ate supper round the fire. The cornmeal pudding was scorched, but Dolly gave them each a dipping from the molasses piggin.

"While it lasts," she had said, "we may as well take what comfort we can get."

Her gloom and Joel's anxiety seemed to settle on the room like a heavy film. Marguerite felt suddenly old and tired, as far removed from the girl who had danced to Seth Jordan's fiddle as if that had been fifty years ago and not the day before. A score of taunting remarks that Caleb had made to her of late came back to prick painfully at her mind. "You—why, you're next thing to an Injun," he had flung at her again and again. "You're French!" She sighed and tried to put the memory from her by forcing her fingers faster at the knitting.

And then, out of the noise of the storm, there came another sound outside the door—a faint scratching, and then the thud of something flung against the logs. They all started up, listening.

"Something is trying to get in!" cried Marguerite.

"That's right," came from Ira. "It's at the other side now."

"Pumpkin!" Jacob sprang up from the floor where he had been lying half-asleep, "Pumpkin's come back!"

"Can't be—he'd bark," said Caleb.

They all followed Ira to the door while he unbolted it a crack and peered out, taking care to keep one hand on his musket.

"Watch out!" Dolly told them sharply. "You keep away from that door."

But there was no need of her warning, for suddenly a yellow head was poked through the narrow opening, and a thin and dripping Pumpkin wriggled in between's Ira's legs.

"Pumpkin! I knew 'twas Pumpkin!" cried Jacob, flinging his arms about the dog's wet fur.

"Pauvre chien! Pauvre chien!" Marguerite was on her knees beside him.

He had started towards them bravely enough with tail waving, but he fell exhausted at Marguerite's feet, the ribs showing sharply under his water-soaked coat. In an instant she had taken his head into her lap, and her hands were busied with the matted fur.

"Quick," she told the children, "get me water and—and a knife. No," as Jacob cried out at this," "no, I shall not harm him, but he is hurt. See what they have done to him!"

No wonder he had not been able to bark. His jaws were tightly bound together with stout leather thongs. His muzzle showed raw and bloody where he had tried to paw them loose. Besides this an ugly open gash showed in his side, and the fur about his neck was half rubbed away as if from trying to slip a noose.

"Poor old fellow," said Ira. "He looks as if they'd 'most done for him."

The children stood about crying, and Marguerite felt tears in her own already smarting eyes.

"Look," Jacob cried between sobs. "He's waggin' of his tail—he's tryin' to."

"Well, he's got home anyhow," Caleb was saying with unusual show of feeling. "There, now I've got those leather bands off'n him, he can drink."

But the dog's tongue was too swollen with thirst for him to move it. Marguerite dipped water in her hands and let it trickle down his throat, and he rolled his eyes up to her gratefully.

Dolly seemed almost as much moved by Pumpkin's return as the children. She brought out some of the salve Aunt Hepsa had given them for Jacob's cut and a few hoarded scraps of cloth to bind up his wounds.

"Wisht I had some milk to give him," Becky said.

"He needs more'n milk," Ira answered, returning from the cupboard with the metal flask he always wore slung over one shoulder when he went on hunting expeditions. He poured a little from this down the dog's throat, and it seemed to revive him somewhat.

"I count every drop as dear as silver," he told Marguerite and the children, "but I don't begrudge it to him. No, sir. Any dog that's come through what he has deserves as much as a human."

Marguerite dressed his hurts as well as she could and

made a warm bed for him by the fire. Jacob begged to sleep beside him, and it was only when Ira promised to come down in the night and administer more from the flask that the child was willing to turn in with the rest under the covers.

Pumpkin recovered in time, though he always had a stiff hind leg to show for the experience. The scar was still plain on his side, and sometimes when he twitched or gave little barks in his sleep, Marguerite wondered if he might not be dreaming himself a captive once more.

"If dogs could talk," she would say to the children, "Pumpkin would have much to tell us."

Though the immediate danger of an Indian raid had waned, the whole household still kept sharp lookout, and Joel and Ira decided not to risk another search for the cave and its secret.

"We'd gain nothin' if we did find it," they told each other. "Brindle an' her calf are gone. Findin' their bones somewhere won't fetch 'em back."

Of their neighbors they saw little now that the cold had set in. Even Ira had small chance to go to see Abby Welles, though Joel and Dolly Sargent complained that he would leave them to do the chores alone any day the wind happened to be right for sailing up the eastern channel towards the Welleses'. That he and Abby were pledged to one another had been taken for granted by everyone since the day of the corn-shelling, but there seemed no likelihood of their marrying for a year at least. Ira had taken over a small part of his brother's claim. He owned a hundred-acre strip beyond their eastern point, but not a tree had been felled as yet and no cellar or well dug.

"It's small wonder Hannah Welles hates the sight o'

me," Ira said to Dolly once in Marguerite's hearing. "She was set on Abby takin' up with Ethan."

"There's no denyin' he's got a lot to offer her," she answered, "with the whole o' Sunday Island comin' to him an' plenty o' room for all under Seth's roof."

"She'll never regret lovin' me," Marguerite heard Ira reply as he took up his ax and went out to the pile of logs.

It was a fairly warm day for December, and she went out with Debby to watch him split the wood. It was pleasant to see his ax come down so swift and sure each time, and sometimes when he paused to rest he would talk to her for a minute or two. The baby was so well wrapped in a woolen shawl that she looked like a brownish caterpillar with a pink nose and tufts of light hair showing at one end.

"What time of year is it now?" Marguerite asked as Ira stopped to draw his sleeve across his streaming forehead.

"Let's see," he answered going over to the post where he still made his daily notches, dividing the months by means of long horizontal strokes. "Well, I declare, if it ain't got to be the middle o' December! Yes, tomorrow's the seventeenth, time I finished that beaver cap I promised Abby."

"Is it for Christmas?" asked Marguerite.

But he shook his head. "No," he said. "Our folks don't hold with such foolishness. We went to meetin' back in Marblehead on Christmas, I recollect, but there was a Dutch boy I knew told me how they had all kinds o' doin's where he come from."

"You mean, it will be no different from other days?" Marguerite's eyes grew wide with disappointment. "No carols, and no cakes, and no gifts from one to another?"

"I guess that's about right," he told her and went on with the chopping.

If Ira gave her no encouragement in Christmas festivities she knew it would be useless to expect more of Dolly and Joel Sargent. She tried to put the thought from her mind, but as each day came bringing it nearer she found herself remembering more and more the happy preparations for it she had helped to make at home. She dreamed of the Christmas cakes Grand'mère had always baked with such pride, of the seeded raisins and the picked nutmeats stirred ceremoniously in the rich batter. And then there were the carols, with the Sisters in the convent beating time and making sure that not a single "Noël" was left out when all their pupils' voices were lifted together. She tried to tell the children of the tiny carved statues of the Virgin and Joseph and the little Christ Child in the manger, with cattle and sheep and shepherds all painted as perfectly as life, that were brought out on Christmas Eve in the candlelit chapel. Unfortunately Dolly had overheard part of this recital and had chided her roundly.

"I'll thank you to keep your Popishness to yourself," she had told her. "We may be in too godforsaken a spot for a meetin' house, but that's no reason to put ideas in the children's heads."

And so it came to be Christmas Eve in the log cabin on Sargents' point with no smell of spice cakes, or incense, or candles, and none to feel the lack of them but Marguerite Ledoux.

She had been out to the post herself that noon, counting the month's notchings to be sure. There could be no doubt—tomorrow would make twenty-five. She would not have missed the holiday preparations so much, she thought, if she might have gone over to see Aunt Hepsa; but she knew there was no chance of this with such a high sea running and snow left in patches from last week's fall. It was rare, Joel had said, to have much fall near the sea. A bad winter ahead, Seth Jordan had predicted, and it looked as if he was right. Frost had covered the little square panes of glass with such feathery patternings, it required much breathing and scratching to make even a little hole to see out. Marguerite was tired of doing this. The room was almost dark, but she knew that outside there was still half an hour or so left of twilight. She went over to the pegs behind the door and took down the brown cloak and hood.

"What are you doin'?" Dolly asked her as she had her hand on the door.

"I'm—I want to bring more cones," she hazarded, grasping at the first idea that came into her head. "There are not so many left in the basket."

"Well, all right, then," Dolly told her, "only don't fetch in the wet ones that make the fire smoke. Pick 'em from underneath. No, Jacob," she added at a question from the child, "you can't go along—it's too cold.

Marguerite buckled on the shoes Aunt Hepsa had given her, tied on her cloak, and went out, basket in hand. Once she shut the door behind her some of the depression which had weighed upon her spirit all day left her. It was impossible to feel so sad out in the snow with the pointed trees and all their shiny dark-green needles. They smelled of Christmas to her. There had been branches of evergreen in the chapel sometimes. Perhaps if she hunted at the edge of the tall woods behind the spring she might find some red partridge berries to bring back to the children. It was bad luck if you gave nothing on Christmas, and they need not know the reason for such a gift.

As she turned into the wood path behind the house she looked across the water to Sunday Island. White places showed on the cleared field round the Jordan house where the snow remained, and the trees above it on the upper pasture where she and Aunt Hepsa had gathered bayberry looked more dark and bristling than ever in the winter twilight. She was glad that a curl of smoke rose from the chimney. Aunt Hepsa must be cooking supper, she told herself, and she paused to send her a Christmas wish across the water.

"I wonder if she's begun her new quilt yet?" she thought as she struck into the wood path. "She had the indigo dye Ethan brought her all ready to make a blue pot."

There were no red berries under the snow in the clearing by the spring where she had hoped to find them, so she went on farther along the blazed trail. It was very still there, with only a light wind stirring the spruce and fir boughs overhead. The light stayed longer there than she had expected, for the snow helped prolong the winter afternoon. Sometimes she stooped to gather cones, taking care to shake off the snow as Dolly Sargent had bidden her. The cold was intense, but her blood was quick and the old homespun cloak and hood enveloped her warmly. There was no sound except her footfalls in the snow. A sudden impulse came upon her to sing one of the carols which she knew the Sisters in the convent must even then be teaching other voices to raise.

She set down the half-filled basket of cones, folded her hands piously under the cloak, and began the first simple little chant that she had ever learned.

"*Noël——Noël——Noël!*"

Her own voice startled her in the stillness. Then at the sound of the familiar words she grew confident and began the one that had been Grand'mère's favorite because she also had sung it when she was a girl in the little village where she had lived.

> *J'entends le ciel retentir*
> *Des cantiques des Saints Anges,*
> *Et la terre tressaillir*
> *Des transports de leurs louanges.*
> *C'est l'Oinct qui devoit venir,*
> *Il est déjà dans ses langes.*
> *Miracle! prodige nouveau,*
> *Le fils de Dieu dans le berceau!*
> *Mais plus grand prodige encore,*
> *Ce grand Roi, que le ciel adore*
> *Doit expirer sur un poteau.*
> *Noël! Noël! Noël!* *

As she sang there in the deepening twilight, she felt strangely comforted. The French words that had lain so long forgotten welled up out of her mind as easily as if she

---

* This old carol may be freely rendered as follows:—

> I hear the heavens resound
> To such angelic song
> That trembling stirs the ground,
> While rolls the news along.
> The Heavenly Child is found,
> To Whom all praise belong.
> Oh! wondrous miracle,
> A God in his cradle!
> Yet must we wonder more,
> This King the heavens adore
> Must die upon a cross.

had been with the Sisters in the candlelit chapel and not alone these thousands of miles away in a snowy wood.

"Noël! Noël!" she cried once more to the ranks of spruces, and then as she turned to retrace her steps something dark and swift moved toward her from behind a tree trunk.

There was not time enough to run away. The words were hardly cool on her lips before he stood beside her—a tall Indian in skins, with a musket that went oddly with his fringes and bright feathers. So silently did he come that not a twig snapped under his foot. He seemed not to dent the snow as he moved over it. His eyes showed bright in the copper of his skin, and a deep scar ran crookedly across one cheek. He came so close that she saw it plainly, and yet she could not move so much as an inch. Her feet seemed rooted in the snow, and if her heart continued to beat, she could not feel it. For what seemed like ages he continued to regard her fixedly with his black, unblinking eyes, while she waited for him to seize the tomahawk from his belt and make an end of her. But he did not move to do so. Instead, his lips parted in a queer smile.

"Noël!" he said, pronouncing the word carefully in a deep, gutteral voice. "Noël!"

Marguerite felt her heart begin to beat again, though her knees were still numb and she continued to stare at him incredulously. Surely this must be a miracle, more extraordinary than any bestowed on Saint Catherine or Saint Elizabeth! A savage had come out of the woods to greet her in her own tongue on Christmas Eve! She forced herself to smile back and answer him.

His words were meager and hard to catch, but she made

out from them and his signs that he had lived with the French in Quebec. He was bound there now, or so she guessed from his pointing finger. She could not tell how many of her words he understood, but whenever she said "Noël" his eyes would brighten with recognition and he would repeat it after her. "Les Pères Gris," he told her, had cured him. He touched the scar as he spoke and crossed his two lean forefingers to make a cross.

It was almost dark now; only a faint light lingered between the spruces. Pumpkin barked in the distance, and Marguerite knew she must hurry back lest they grow alarmed. What would they think, Joel and Dolly Sargent and the rest, if they should come upon her there in the woods holding converse with an Indian? Prompted by an impulse she pulled the cord out from under her dress and jerked off Oncle Pierre's gilt button. It glittered in her hand as she held it out to the tall figure before her.

"Pour un souvenir de Noël," she said as she laid it in his hand before she turned and sped off toward the clearing.

Her heart was still pounding as she came out of the woods and in sight of the log house. Pumpkin bounded to meet her as she paused to put back the cord and its only remaining treasure. She had not thought to make such a Christmas gift, but surely she could not have done less. She could not but feel that somehow it was a fortunate sign, this strange meeting. Perhaps Le Bon Dieu had Himself arranged it that she might be less lonely on Christmas Eve. But she knew there must not be a word of it to the rest. She would never be able to make them understand what she scarcely understood herself. As for Caleb, she could well guess what he would say and that he would think ill of her ever after.

Dolly Sargent scolded her roundly for staying away so long.

"I declare you deserve a beatin'," she told her hotly, "strayin' so far at this time o' night. I vow Debby's got more sense 'n you show sometimes."

There was no mention made of Christmas next day save that Joel asked a lengthier blessing over their breakfast cornmeal than was usual with him. But Marguerite no longer minded. Had she not had her miracle the night before?

Seth Jordan's predictions for the winter were more than surpassed. It is still remembered in those parts by old men and women who recall tales their grandparents and great-grandparents told of its bitterness. Snow fell as it had not in many seasons before, and no sooner would the sun appear and a slight thaw set in than this would be followed by spells of cold which made a crust heavy enough to bear a man's weight. Northeast winds blew continuously, with sleet that cut like fine wires. It was impossible to put out in the boats in such weather; and then in February the channel froze over solid. This happened after a week of such bitter cold that during those seven days the Sargent family had burned up more than half their winter's supply of firewood. Joel and Ira would be up every other hour of the night throwing on more logs, and it was only by placing quilts and featherbeds on the floor nearby that the family were able to sleep in comfort.

"Beats any cold I ever knew," Ira said as he reported on the frozen channel. "I lay by another day we could drive a team across to Sunday Island."

" 'Twould be pretty hard goin' with the twelve-foot tide hereabouts," his brother told him. "Still, even if the ice was pretty rough I s'pose a body could do it safely."

The children were all eagerness to try. It would be fine, they thought, to surprise Aunt Hepsa by making a visit to her on foot. But their mother would not hear of such a thing, and even Ira said he would let someone else cross it first.

Food was none too plenty on the Sargent table in those days. They were down to dried fish and scrapings of corn-meal from the bottom of the barrel, with a few of their own turnips. It was poor fare with no more molasses to sweeten it.

"Maybe it's as well we lost Brindle and her calf," sighed Dolly. "They'd never have lasted through such a spell, an' I couldn't bear to see 'em starvin'. It's hard enough with the children gettin' puny right under my eyes."

Marguerite had not noticed this before, but now that it was pointed out to her she realized that they all looked pale and spindling. They had lost their freckles and summer sunburn during the weeks indoors, and their eyes showed bigger and rounder than before. Jacob in particular appeared scrawny and pinched. He looked like a wizened little old man in the baggy jacket and breeches of gray wool.

"He's been limsy ever since that hammer hit him," his mother told Joel. "I declare I don't know what to dose him with."

"He'll pick up come spring," he had assured her.

"If it ever does come spring," Ira had put in from the corner.

Marguerite, dandling Debby on her lap, could not help

agreeing with Ira. A thin patch of winter sunshine came through the frosted panes of the narrow window, and the child reached out her hands as if she would hold it close. She was growing into a little girl now that she was past a year, with a number of small white teeth and fair rings of hair. Already the twins were concerned that she had not begun to talk, but their mother said she could do with less noise about the house for a good while to come.

"Wonder what she'll say first?" Becky questioned.

" '*Ma*', most likely," Susan told her, "or '*baby*,' perhaps. See, '*baby*,' " and she held up the corncob doll as she spoke.

But Debby had notions of her own when it came to talking.

"Maggie," she said quite slowly and distinctly that afternoon as they sat together by the window.

"Well, I never!" exclaimed Dolly Sargent when she heard. "I'll let her have the molasses spoon to suck, just for that!"

Years afterwards Marguerite could not recall Debby's little voice saying her name without wanting to cry, for that very night as they lay sleeping her cries and Pumpkin's barks were to rouse them. A strong northeast wind had risen with evening and that, added to the intense cold, had driven them to spreading their bedding around the fire. They slept in a half-circle about it, the two men and Caleb at either end; Dolly, Marguerite, and the children in the middle. She had Patty and Jacob beside her under the Rose of Sharon quilt, with the twins huddled between her and their mother and Debby. Already Joel and Ira had been up replenishing the fire by turns. Marguerite had half-wakened at the thud of the logs being thrown on. She had peered out sleepily once to see Ira pushing them far back against the chimney to safeguard against sparks.

And then there came that terrible crying. She started up from sleep to see Debby crawling on the hearthstone, her dress a mass of flames, and Pumpkin leaping frantically in circles about her, tearing at the burning stuff with his teeth. Marguerite could not move nor utter a sound. She saw Dolly catch up the blazing bundle and beat the flames fiercely with her bare hands before Joel seized the nearest bed cover to smother the fire. Ira had run for the water bucket. He was dousing the child with it, cursing the dog who still leaped under foot. Between them they had it out in a few minutes, but the harm was done.

They gathered in a frightened group about the child. Dolly held her close, trying as gently as possible to peel off the charred cloth of the dress and old shawl.

"Don't seem as if she could've slipped out without I felt her," she kept repeating, "but she must 'a' done it somehow an' crawled right into the fire. I'd wrapped her up in the shawl for warmth. I never thought how easy the fringes could catch. Oh, Joel, what'll we do for her?"

"If we had sweet oil or butter to smear on, 'twould help," Ira was saying. "Here, Dolly, give her to me while you get what's left o' that salve."

But there was so little of it, and Debby's burns were so many. They seemed to reach from head to foot of her little body. It was terrible to see her so swollen and blackened and to hear her moaning as the pain increased. Marguerite felt her own tears wet on her cheeks and to her astonishment she saw Caleb turn away from the rest as if he could not bear the sight.

"It's our fault," Dolly was crying to her husband wildly. "Yours for bringin' us to such a pass, an' mine for not doin' as Hepsa Jordan said. But I didn't have the heart to brand her against the fire, an' now look what it's done to her! Look at her, Joel Sargent, just look at her!"

He took the baby and began to pace the room with her in his arms. It seemed to ease the child a little for her cries grew fainter. Marguerite had never seen Joel Sargent look like this before, his face suddenly broken and twitching.

Ira and Dolly were mixing water with a cupful of white flour that she had kept hoarded. They would spread this on the burns and make it go as far as they could. Jacob and Patty and the twins sat huddled by the settle, crying softly together in fright and sympathy.

"Maggie," whispered Becky between her sobs, "Debby ain't goin' to die, is she?"

"Hush," Marguerite told them, "you must not cry."

"But you're cryin' yourself," put in Susan.

"You must be very good and quiet," Marguerite went on, "till I come back."

"But where are you goin' to?" they asked her curiously.

She did not wait to tell them. Instead she ran to Caleb, all her usual dread of him gone in the stress of the moment.

"Caleb," she said, "we must get Aunt Hepsa. She will know what to do."

He stared at her without speaking and she hurried on.

"It is frozen over—all the way. They said the ice would bear us. Only today you heard them say so. Let us go. Quick!" Then as Debby's moans grew worse again, "We must not delay."

"Yes," he answered and she saw his eyes light up with determination, "we'll go."

Marguerite never remembered how they got into their things and out of the house. She only knew they were making their way to the cove by the light of the winter stars and a lantern Caleb had lighted with one of the bayberry candles. It gave out a feeble glow, the light coming in points through piercings in the tin top and sides. She stumbled on a stump and would have fallen but for the hand he reached out to her.

"You'd best keep a-holt," he said, and she was glad to cling to him.

They struggled on together in the teeth of the wind which swept bitterly down the frozen channel. It whipped at Marguerite's cloak so that she was obliged to clutch the folds close with her free hand. It was the darkest time of the night, and their lantern made but shifting points of brightness to guide them over the ice, which had appeared flat from shore but which they found to be rough where the tides and undertow had broken up the earlier layers. They were continually scrambling over these jagged places, slipping and catching themselves, only to go stumbling again. Sometimes they had to work their way around gaps in the ice piles, or jump over hollows and frozen gullies. A fear that they might be going in circles came over Marguerite, for it was all so black she could not distinguish the outlines of either Sunday Island or their own shore. Then she saw Caleb's head turned again and again to the sky. She knew he was following the tip of the Great Dipper, and she thanked God fervently that there was no sign of fog. If they could keep their footing and those stars directly before them they must reach the Island, unless— But she would not think of such a possibility. Ira had said the ice was solid, even in the middle where so long there had been a narrow passage of open water.

They had not breath enough to speak to one another if they could have made themselves heard. The wind whistled in their ears, and there were terrifying creakings as the waters below strained against the ice barriers. Marguerite shuddered to hear it as they pressed on, her feet like frozen clods as she forced them forward, her hands numb and aching in her woolen mittens. Once they stopped to change places that Caleb might shift the lantern to his other hand.

"We're 'most halfway," he shouted to her as he did so, stamping to try and bring back some feeling to his feet.

Once more they were plunging on. Marguerite stumbled and fell to her knees, but Caleb pulled her up again. Her leg hurt where she had struck it; still she forced herself forward, her breath coming in short gasps.

Now they were on a smoother stretch, where it seemed they could feel the tug of the tide under the ice. The lantern flickered feebly, and they could barely make out a foot-length ahead. Any weak places would be here, they knew. Instinctively they drew closer, feeling their way cautiously step by step. But it held firmly under them, and when they felt the rougher places once more they knew that the most dangerous part was past. On and on they toiled, now slipping, now righting one another, now stopping to gain breath enough to struggle on a few more yards.

And so they came within sight of their goal. The sky to the eastward showed faintly gray, and no sight had ever seemed more welcome to them than the dark shoreline of Sunday Island.

"We're 'most there," Caleb managed to gasp, but Marguerite had no breath to answer him.

There was a dull pain about her heart, and every breath hurt her cruelly. She had long since ceased to have any feeling in her hands or feet.

"I can't go on. I can't!" something in her seemed to be crying out. "Another step will be the end of me."

Then she would remember Debby's crying and Dolly's despair and press on. If it had not been for Caleb she could never have climbed the last steep pitch before they reached the Jordan house. But he half dragged her to the doorstep, where she sank in a heap.

If they had been two ghosts Hepsa and Seth and Ethan Jordan could not have been more startled to find them there, Caleb beating with frost-numbed knuckles on the doorframe, and Marguerite by his side.

"In God's name," the old woman was saying as she drew them in to the fire and began to pull off their outerthings, "how did you two young ones ever do it?"

Marguerite was too spent to tell her. She had not even strength to help Caleb explain their plight. She knew he was telling them about Debby while the old woman rubbed her hands and feet and Seth and Ethan did the same to his.

"So we came to you," she heard Caleb saying, "to get you to come an' help her."

"But, Hepsa," Marguerite knew Seth was very serious, though she could not lift her head to see his face, "you can't go out there across the ice. You give me what they need an' Ethan an' I'll take it."

"I'm a-goin' too," she heard the old woman answer firmly. "I guess if those young ones could do it, I can. You get the wood sled out, Ethan, an' I'll be ready."

Presently Aunt Hepsa was bending over her, pouring something hot and stinging down her throat.

"Carry her in to my bed, Seth," she heard her say. "They'll be safe here till we can get back."

She felt warm covers being wrapped about her. The iron screws that had been tightening with every breath she drew began to lessen and she felt a queer lightness and ease steal over her.

"You will not let her die?" she whispered faintly.

"I'll do my best, child," she heard Hepsa answer as she drifted off to sleep.

But Aunt Hepsa's best was not enough. Neither was Marguerite's and Caleb's.

It was past noon before they returned again over the ice, the old woman on the sled with Seth and Ethan dragging it after them. Caleb was up, limping about the kitchen on frostbitten toes, and Marguerite had wakened faint and sore under the covers. They knew before any of the three spoke what had happened.

"We done all we could," Aunt Hepsa told them at last as she stooped to warm herself at the fire Caleb had replenished, "but she was 'most gone when we got there."

"You mean she's—she's *dead?*" Caleb's voice sounded thin and hollow as he put the question.

"Yes, poor little mite," Aunt Hepsa answered, "an' I expect 'tis better so, for she couldn't ever be cured o' such burns as those. Only I can't seem to reconcile it no way."

"But she was too little to die!" Marguerite's tears were hot on her cheeks. "She was good and happy and—and she said my name, just yesterday she did, all by herself."

She flung herself face down among the pillows, crying wildly in her grief and weakness, while the old lady sat beside her, touching her heaving shoulders with a kindly hand.

"Then 'twas all for nothin'," she heard Caleb say slowly, "our comin' across the channel an' all."

"I'm afraid so, boy," Seth answered. "Put on your things an' I'll haul you back on the sled. There's plenty for all hands to do over there, an' praise be the ice holds."

After the men had gone over again, Aunt Hepsa made a strong brewing of herb tea which she and Marguerite drank steaming from the kettle. That put new strength in them both, and when the old woman brought out a length of soft woolen cloth Marguerite was able to help her sew it into Debby's last little dress.

"I'd a piece o' linen, too," Hepsa Jordan said as they worked, "but some way I couldn't bear to put that on her in this bitter weather. I expect we always think the dead go on feelin' even when we know they can't no more."

"Yes," sighed Marguerite, "and she'd have looked so pretty in this. It's almost white. She never had any but gray holland or linsey before."

Seth had fashioned a little box out of planks he had brought over, and Ethan helped Joel dig the grave in a cleared patch at the edge of the woods. It was hard work cutting even so small a place in the frozen ground. Their axes and spades rang out dully as if they were striking stone instead of earth. Marguerite heard them as she and Aunt Hepsa and Ira came over the ice next day.

There were not shoes and wraps enough to go round, so Marguerite stayed indoors with the younger ones while the rest did what must be done. Caleb told her later that they had said a prayer, but that even Aunt Hepsa couldn't raise a hymn tune, it was so cold.

That night they were all too tired to talk, and even Dolly had no more tears to shed.

It was only by the next afternoon that Marguerite could get her swollen feet into her shoes and limp as far as the little grave. It looked a very small mound, even for Debby, and she stood beside it to make a prayer of her own. Pumpkin had followed her out. He crouched beside the place, his tail drooping, his wise brown eyes sad, as if he too were mourning. When she had said all the prayers she could remember, she still lingered. The wind blew sharp from the sea and already what sunlight there had been was going fast. Once more Marguerite folded her hands that were still sore and frostbitten and sang the little lullaby she had so often rocked Debby to sleep by:—

> *Do, do, l'enfant do,*
> *L'enfant dormira bientôt.*
> *Do, do l'enfant do,*
> *L'enfant dormira tantôt.*

As she turned to go back to the house with Pumpkin at her heels, she saw the sun going down behind the islands. Long yellow fingers of light were spreading over the western sky. Ira had come out to cut another notch on the post by the door.

"Tomorrow'll be the first o' March," he told her with one of his rare, slow smiles. "I guess we'll none of us mind seein' the last o' winter."

PART 4   SPRING

The Spring thaw was a long while in coming. In spite of Ira's notches on the post it seemed there would be no end to snow and sleet and steady northeast blows. The ice had long since broken up in the channel, but crossing was now more difficult because of shifting masses of it and because of heavy seas. Ira had not seen Abby in weeks, and this irked him.

"If there was any sort o' trail blazed near shore I could make the Welles place easy in half a day's walkin'," he complained to Dolly.

"You'd wear it into a road soon enough if there was," she told him. "To hear you take on, anybody'd think that girl was goin' to be gray an' toothless 'fore you saw her again!"

"Does seem like years since I set eyes on her," he sighed and went back to the wooden bucket he was fashioning against sap-taking time.

For a long while now they had been talking of the two sugar maples in the half-cleared land near the spring and of the fine syrup they could soon have to sweeten their hasty pudding.

"My mouth fair hankers for a taste of it," Ira told the

children as he hollowed out wooden pegs to drive into the trees. "But I guess we'd best wait till the Line storm's past. That's due 'bout now."

It came as he had predicted. The log house rocked on its foundations to the winds that raged for upwards of two days and nights. Marguerite marveled to hear them tell of it and of how all this tumult meant that far away to the south the sun was crossing the equator. All this commotion that the days and nights might be of equal length, and then slowly the days would grow longer and warmer, and it would be summer again.

"How marvelous is the sun," she thought. "No wonder that people worshiped it in olden days as Oncle Pierre told me."

She found this tree-tapping very strange and mysterious. In Le Havre she had never heard of such doings. Her curious questionings amused Ira and rekindled Caleb's scorn, which had been noticeably less since they had shared the dangers of that expedition over the ice to Sunday Island. She had to be reassured many times that it would not kill the maple trees to drive in the spouts and rob them of the sap.

There was much excitement in the house when the day for this came round, for the melting snow and ice made walking difficult, and there were not enough shoes for all the young Sargents. The twins drew lots to see which should wear their one pair, and Patty was inconsolable over her lack of any till Marguerite promised to carry her there on her back. So off they set, a queer little procession in the noon sunshine, with Ira and Caleb at the head bearing hammers, pegs, and wooden pails. They began with the larger of the two maple trees. First Ira cut a place in the bark, then he drove an awl in nearly to the hilt.

"Plenty o' sap there," he told the little group about him. "Give me a spout to ram in, Caleb."

When they were done with the tapping, two large wooden buckets hung from either tree, the sap beginning to drip with a steady *tap-tap* on the bottom almost before they were fastened in place.

"Umm, it's good!" cried Jacob, catching a drop on his finger and smacking his lips over the taste. "It's as sweet as sugar water."

"Just you wait," said Caleb. "It'll be better 'n molasses an' 'most as thick when we get it boiled down."

"It takes a powerful lot to make a pitcherful," warned Ira, "so you young ones have got to come up here every so often to see it don't overflow."

"Yes," agreed Marguerite, "it would be terrible to lose one precious drop."

By the following noon the largest iron pot was full to the brim, ready to be set to boil over a fire that Joel had kindled between stones not far from the house. It was too heavy and hot work to be done indoors, and he had rigged up three stout poles, tent-fashion, from which the kettle might swing by its chain. Dolly came out to stir it with a wooden spoon which Ira had bound to a long piece of wood so that she need not come too near the heat or have her face filled with smoke and steam. Already a cloud of this was rising as the sap began to boil, filling the air with a rich, yet delicate fragrance which tantalized the children, who had gathered on the nearby woodpile. They perched like brown birds or squirrels on the logs, watching with bright eyes; wrinkling their noses in eager expectation.

Under Ira's direction, Marguerite and Caleb filled a flat pan with clean, fresh snow from the woods, packing it down firmly into a solid mass. They set this beside the waiting wooden piggin, and when Dolly said the syrup was done, and Joel and Ira lifted off the kettle on a stout pole and set it aside, the great moment had come. Great ladles full of the seething brown liquid were now poured over the pan of packed snow, the syrup hardening in a fragrant, sugary crust, while the rest was poured steaming into the piggin.

"Come on an' help yourselves," Ira bade the children, setting the pan down on the top log and breaking off a huge chunk for himself.

Never, thought Marguerite, had anything tasted so delicious! After the months of salt fish, cornmeal, and turnips it seemed like some unbelievable magic fare with its sweetness and flavor. Even Joel and Dolly joined in the exclamations of pleasure at each mouthful, and the children soon were brown and sticky with all they had eaten.

"It is well this is not summer," laughed Marguerite at Jacob's and Patty's smeared faces and hands, "or the bees would be swarming about you, you are so sweet!"

They chuckled at the idea, licking their fingers clean of the last bit.

Afternoon was waning by the time they were done. Dolly marshaled the children indoors again, but Marguerite went with Ira to bring down the fresh sap from the maples. He carried the large bucket and she the smaller, and the trees showed dark against a pale yellow sky as they went up together.

Involuntarily Marguerite stopped as they passed Debby's little mound.

" 'Tis a shame she never had a taste of maple sugar," she said sadly; "she was that fond of sweet things."

Ira did not speak, but she knew from his quiet nod that he felt as she did. As they came down carrying the full buckets he squinted off at the Mount Desert hills and the northeast sky.

"Wind's gettin' more westerly," he told her. "If it holds like this I've a notion to go over to the Welles place. Want to go along?"

Marguerite flushed with eager gratefulness. "But I do not know," she hastened to add, "whether Dolly can spare me from the house and the children."

"I'll see to that," he assured her, then he added somewhat sheepishly, "I reckon Abby'd like for you to teach her some o' those fancy stitches you learned over in France. You don't have no use for 'em here, an' Abby's got aplenty of cloth to work on."

Marguerite lay awake long that night, wondering if Dolly would make objections to this plan. But she raised little more than a complaint or two, only charging them to be back early in time to help her with the sap and syrup kettles. The children clamored to go when they saw her putting her shoes on over her moccasins and tying on the brown cloak.

"You can save your breath," Ira told them good-naturedly, at the same time including Caleb in his remark. "Maggie's the only crew I'm takin'."

He had the dory ready when she ran down to the cove, and he had fetched along a small bucket of the syrup and some fine squirrel and otter skins he had been curing as presents. The wind was fresh but not too chill, and the sun danced on the edge of every wave.

"This breeze'll serve us pretty," said Ira, pushing out before he hoisted the triangle of canvas to their spruce-pole mast. "Seems like we could commence to count on spring at last, though April's still ahead, an' that's a treacherous month."

It was strange and delightful being out in the dory with Ira. He did not talk much, but that was no matter with the wind from a proper quarter and so much of joyful anticipation ahead. Ira whistled as he let out and shifted sail, making use of one of the oars for rudder from the stern seat. He seemed happier, Marguerite thought, than on any day since his last visit before Christmas. She had never been in that direction and it filled her with zest to see each wooded point they passed and to mark how the shapes of the Mount Desert hills changed from this slightly nearer view. They seemed darker and more deeply indented than from their own land. Marguerite tried to keep the outlines fixed in her mind. It would be pleasant to have them there long after she was back on the Sargent point.

"There 'tis," said Ira suddenly after they had been sailing some time; "just past the point."

Marguerite found herself possessed with curiosity to see this other home, and at the same time with a deep shyness. She remembered Hannah Welles' frowns and her often disapproving tongue on the occasions of the Raising and the corn-shelling; and she could not help thinking how worn and dingy her own brown homespun would look beside Abby's clean, bright dresses. Just for a moment she wished she might go back. But it was too late for such regrets; already the square, weathered house with its low roof and sheds had come into view, patches of snow still showing in the clearing and woods behind.

They could hear the sound of chopping from this direction as they neared shore. Ira furled the sail and rowed the dory in with long, strong strokes. The shore made a natural little harbor roundabout, a more quiet, sheltered place than their cove, but shallower. Ira said that no vessel as large as the *Isabella B.* could have anchored there. When they were halfway in he lifted up his voice in a great halloo which brought two figures to the door. One of these, heavy and in dark skirts, Marguerite recognized as Hannah Welles, and the other she knew at once for Abby. In another moment Abby was hurrying down toward shore to welcome them, bareheaded, with her blue skirts blowing about her as she ran.

"Ira," she called when they were within hailing distance, "I've been lookin' for you this long time!"

She sent the pebbles rattling down the little beach as she came running to the place where Ira dragged the dory up. He put Marguerite and the things ashore carefully before he caught her up in his arms, holding her there as easily as if she had been Patty.

"No, no you mustn't," she protested. "Mother's got her eye to the window, an' you know how she feels!"

"I know," said Ira with a headshake, setting her down again and walking beside her toward the house.

Marguerite followed them up the path. She felt a little in awe of this girl who, though she might be only five years older, was so far removed from her by reason of the feelings she had awakened in Ira and Ethan Jordan. She could not hear what Ira was saying, but she knew he smiled often as he bent over Abby's brown, blowing hair.

The family in the gray board house had seen no outsiders for so long that even Hannah Welles welcomed them warmly. Perhaps she was growing reconciled to Ira and the Sargents, though she still made sharp remarks about his dependence on his brother and about the risk they ran in so stubbornly settling where they had. The bucket of syrup which Ira had fetched brought some show of pleasure into her face. She admitted to having a sweet tooth, and so far they had not discovered any sugar maples on their land. Ira agreed to go up to the wood lot to see how Timothy and Nathan were coming along with the chopping and hauling, and while he was out Marguerite was questioned minutely on all the happenings of the winter.

Seth Jordan had brought them news of Debby's death, but Hannah Welles wanted all the details and made many comments and offered dire warnings of her own. Abby was more sympathetic.

"Poor little thing!" she said. "It don't seem right such things should befall 'em."

After that all three set about preparing dinner. There was much talk and bustle over the addition of a pumpkin pie they had been keeping for some special occasion. Abby felt there could be no doubt that its time had come, though her mother seemed less inclined to share it with Ira Sargent and Marguerite. She gave in at the end, however, and set it to warm in the brick oven. Marguerite's eyes were quite dazzled by all the pieces of pewter and crockery this kitchen boasted. There were not so many as on the Jordans' shelves, but still, after their own meager stock of wooden plates and a cracked bowl or two and one pewter tankard and mug, it seemed a grand sight indeed. As for the set of sprigged china cups and saucers, they were of a shining gayety that quite took her breath away. Hannah saw the admiration in the girl's eyes and shook her head.

"Abby's offered to give 'em back to Ethan," she told her, with a sidewise glance at her daughter's head bent over the mixing trough, "but he told her to keep 'em. I don't hold with takin' gifts from any man but the one a girl's pledged to marry. But Abby's got notions of her own. Well, I wash my hands of the whole business."

"Exceptin' every day when you tell her what a fool she is to take me!" came Ira's voice from the doorway, where he stood tall and smiling.

Once the dinner dishes were cleared away Abby, at Ira's suggestion, brought out the new calico dress she was making and several lengths of material for more—a buff cotton with a pattern of little green leaves scattered over it; another of striped blue and white, and a cloak she was fashioning from several yards of fine red broadcloth which Timothy had brought back from the fall trip. Marguerite's eyes shone as she fingered the rich, crimson folds. She felt a craving for color after the long winter months, just as she had for the sweetness of the maple syrup.

"Father said it was scandalous when Timothy told him what he paid for this," Abby told her, "but it'll be my best for years to come."

"It is the color of red roses," said Marguerite, stroking the smooth folds softly with her finger, "like some that grew in our garden in Le Havre."

"An' you'll look like a rose yourself when you wear it," murmured Ira, with a quick glance to make sure Hannah Welles was busy at the far side of the kitchen. Timothy was waiting impatiently outside to take him down to inspect a new dory he was building near shore, but still Ira lingered, watching Abby unfolding the cloth or holding up the dresses she had already cut and basted.

"I can do plain sewing," Abby was explaining to Marguerite, "but when it comes to fancy stiches for trimmin' I've no notion how to go about it. Ira thought maybe you'd show me some."

Hannah Welles sniffed disapprovingly from her corner and gave it as her opinion that a girl was lucky if she got a calico for summer and a linsey for winter, without worrying her head with fashions and furbelows. Marguerite noticed, however, that when she began to make some of her embroidery stitches on a piece of cotton for Abby to go by, Hannah drew almost as close as her daughter to watch. Marguerite's fingers were a little clumsy after all the heavier work of the winter. The needle and thread seemed too fine at first, then gradually the old patterns came back to her and she found the needle moving in and out with its old cunning.

"It's a wonder to see how you can do it," marveled Abby.

"It is nothing," Margurite told her, flushing with pleasure. "You should see how the Sisters in the convent could make flowers, in wreaths and little garlands, and lace as well. If I had stayed another year I was to learn lace-making."

"A couple o' good patchwork quilts would be a better way to spend the time," observed Hannah Welles.

"Ah, yes," agreed Marguerite. "Aunt Hepsa has promised to help me with one. Already I know the patterns of 'Rose of Sharon' and 'Feathered Star,' and she will show me the 'Delectable Mountains.' "

Abby was quick to learn, and her admiration filled Marguerite with happiness. She forgot her old dress and clumsy shoes; she even forgot, for the afternoon, that she was the Sargents' Bound-out Girl whose French words and ways were a continual source of annoyance to them. There was a little roll of calico snippets left from the dresses which she eyed longingly. The twins' corncob doll was in dire need of new clothing, and she longed to ask Abby for a bit to take home. It was nearly time to leave, however, before she summoned courage to do so, and then she waited till they were alone in the kitchen.

"Why, to be sure you can have a piece," Abby told her kindly. "Here's a bit from my pink print." Then, as she saw the girl's hand reach out to stroke the lengths of broadcloth once more, she continued, "And here's some left over from cuttin' the cloak. It's not enough for a dress or jacket, but maybe you could piece it into a hood for yourself."

Marguerite sat speechless as Abby put the little roll of crimson stuff into her hands. She could not believe such good fortune had befallen her all in one day.

"Oh," she said at last softly, "you are good—good. It warms me through to touch it. It shall be my greatest treasure."

Darkness caught them just as Ira dragged the dory up their own beach. Marguerite's teeth were chattering with the cold of the chill late March evening as she sped up the path, but she knew that under the old brown cloak her hands held a strip of such color as she had not seen since the days in Le Havre. Dolly scolded them less than might have been expected considering the time they had been gone, and when Marguerite showed her the red cloth she offered to let it lie with her own precious scraps and the five pewter spoons she kept in the old pine chest.

Many weeks of raw winds and cold were still before them, but as the days grew steadily longer, all their spirits rose. They had plenty of fresh fish now, and Ira and Joel cut new ax handles and got out all the old tools to be put in readiness against planting time. This was still far off, for even by mid-April the frost was not fully out of the ground, though here and there in sunnier places signs of green were already showing.

"I never knew a place where it took so everlastingly long to warm up," Dolly complained. "It's enough to take the heart out o' anybody!"

"Just you wait," Joel would tell her; " 'tain't like other places. Here, they say, it comes all to once."

What worried the men now was their need of ammunition and seed. The severe winter had obliged them to eat all the corn and potatoes, leaving none for sowing. Then they had been forced to shoot more wild fowl and game than they would otherwise have needed. This had made great inroads into their store of powder. There was not even enough to see them through the summer, and in case of an Indian attack they would be in a dangerous position. Joel's face looked worn and very grim whenever he talked of this in the evening after the younger ones were asleep, and even Ira's pleasant mouth began to grow serious.

"I dassent ask Jordan for no more powder," Joel said wearily. "He's not much better off himself, an' Morse an' Stanley they'd begrudge me so much as a farthing's worth, they're so down on us for settlin' here."

"I guess Timothy Welles would let me have some," Ira put in, "but I hate to ask favors till Abby an' I can get married."

Marguerite heard them still discussing the problem after she stretched herself under the covers. When she had first come to stay with them these moments before sleep had been her time for thinking of home—of Le Havre and Grand'mère and Oncle Pierre and the Sisters in the Convent. Now she suddenly realized that she was thinking to herself in English, not French, and that her mind also turned over and over these matters of their daily life and comfort. It concerned her so much more now to wonder how many potatoes they must raise to keep the household through another winter, and whether there would be many nuts and wild berries to gather that summer. Sometimes she went for days without slipping her finger through the gold ring on its cord around her neck. "Perhaps," she thought, in sudden alarm, "I shall someday forget that I have another name than 'Maggie'!"

It was the end of April now, and fresh green was appearing in some new spot each morning as the children and Marguerite ran out of the log house. Ira and Joel took turns with the plow, while the other tussled with last year's stumps. These had been left to rot all winter and now they must be grubbed out and the holes filled and smoothed over. It was desperately hard work. Sometimes it took a whole day to dislodge one of the larger stumps, even with both men exerting all their strength and the children and Dolly cheering them on from the dooryard.

"It is like pulling the teeth of a giant," Marguerite said as she watched Ira get the iron crowbar under a particu-

larly stubborn root and heave and strain with all his weight
to loosen it. "I would there were a yoke of oxen to help."

"You might's well wish for the moon to come down an'
give me a hand!" Ira retorted as he straightened up painfully and wiped his scarlet face before he went at the
stump again.

"Some year, though, we'll have oxen," chirped Patty
cheerfully.

"Yes," added Becky, "an' a white cat with double
paws."

"I'd rather have Pumpkin!" cried Jacob, throwing himself on the dog and rolling over and over with him on the
soft brown earth.

All the children looked less pale and spindling now,
though they had lost their chubbiness during the winter.
Marguerite noticed from her own shadow that she, too,
had lengthened considerably. Her last year's holland was
almost to her knees and strained across the shoulders and
chest. She could reach to set the wooden platters on the
highest shelf now, where before her fingertips had barely
touched the edge. Aunt Hepsa had remarked on the
change in her the first time she had seen her since Debby's
death.

"My, Maggie," she had exclaimed, "You're growin' like
a weed. Watch out you don't get so brown again this summer, an' by another year you won't hardly know yourself
for the same girl."

The old woman had made a fine start with the new
quilt. Already she had half the patches pieced together.
The buff and deep blue colors made the sharp bold outlines of the pattern stand out with extraordinary clearness.

"Yes," Marguerite had cried out in wondering admiration as Aunt Hepsa had spread the squares before her, "it is true. The jagged points *are* like a mountain range—very blue and dark across the water."

Hepsa Jordan had told her then of the name and its meaning. Marguerite listened eagerly. She had never heard of a book called "Pilgrim's Progress" which the old woman declared was second only to the Holy Bible. A man named John Bunyan had written it long ago in a prison in England. The Jordans owned no copy of it, but Aunt Hepsa could remember most of what had befallen the characters of the story—Christian, Great Heart, Mr. Worldly Wiseman, and the rest. Marguerite and the children had hung spellbound while she recounted it.

"I always did admire the part about the mountains," she had wound up, "but first there was that place called 'Doubting Castle' kept by 'Giant Despair'. 'Twas after they got away from there that they went on till they came to the 'Delectable Mountains' an' found the gardens an' orchards an' fountains of water. It's good to recollect that when I'm piecin'."

Marguerite found herself thinking of this often now that she and the children were out again for long hours in the April weather. She often turned her eyes to the distant line of the Mount Desert hills, remembering all Aunt Hepsa had told her, and it was on one of these occasions that she saw a strange white square looming against them.

"Look," she called to Caleb, who was splitting wood for kindling in the dooryard, "and see this strange thing!"

He left the chopping block to join her, narrowing his blue eyes and pushing the sandy lock of hair off his forehead.

"It's a full-rigged vessel and no mistake," he said in an awed tone. "She's comin' this way."

The twins and Jacob ran toward the house, shouting excitedly as they went. "A full-rigged vessel comin' this way!"

Soon the whole family had gathered on the point to watch. There could be no thought of work with such a sight as this approaching over water that had not held any craft larger than sloops and dories for so long. There was much talk and speculation about it, and Joel and Ira decided that it must be taking the inner course to Boston.

"It's a wonder to me, though," said Ira, "why they wouldn't go outside the islands, unless maybe they're in some kind of trouble an' need to put in along the way."

As it turned out this was exactly the case. Before night the ship was riding anchor in their channel, while the Sargents trooped down to the cove in an excited little group to meet the boatload of men who rowed in. She was a fine, three-masted vessel, with square-cut sails of new canvas, and her name in clear letters along the stern—*Fortunate Star*. But she had not lived up to her name, for already, less than two days out, one of her crew had fallen while climbing aloft to take in sail and suffered painful injury. So the men explained after they had beached their boat. They had come to fill their buckets with fresh water and to see if there was any able-bodied man ashore who would take their mate's place on the voyage to Boston. They would anchor in the Channel that night and be off with the tide in the morning. Marguerite, standing with the children on the outskirts of the little group, saw Ira's face light up in quick response and a look of relief pass between him and Joel and Dolly.

"I'll go with you gladly," he told the men eagerly.

"We're carrying lumber to be delivered to His Majesty's agents," one of the others explained. "The vessel's loaded with the finest pine masts for the Royal Navy."

"And they've need of 'em too," put in another, "for fighting these pesky French and Indians."

Caleb might have taken this occasion to make one of his unpleasant remarks about Marguerite's nationality had it not been that he was absorbed in other matters. Ever since Ira had volunteered to go he had been drawing nearer, his freckled face puckered with anxiety over the proposal he was about to make. At last he blurted it out.

"What about takin' me too?" he asked, his voice squeaky with hopefulness. "I can climb the riggin' an' box the compass an'—"

Shouts of hearty laughter from the men cut him short, and Marguerite saw him grow scarlet to the roots of his red hair.

"What do you say, boys?" one of the older men was asking the rest with an amused twinkle in his eye. "Reckon we could use a boy?"

"You needn't give me no wages," Caleb urged them. "I'll work my hands an' feet off to go."

"You can come along back an' talk to the master 'bout it," they told him. "That is, if your folks'll let you."

Joel hesitated at first, but Ira took Caleb's side. He maintained there would be two of them to fetch back supplies from Boston. Besides, it was a chance for the boy to gain seafaring experience on a first-class vessel. Caleb listened to this discussion of his fate, shifting his weight from one bare foot to the other while he waited for the word to be given. Joel had counted on help from Ira and Caleb that spring, and now the possibility of losing them both at once presented grave difficulties. Of course, he vowed, Ira must go. It was too good a chance to get the much-needed ammunition and stores, but Caleb, if he remained, could be very helpful in plowing and sowing. On the other hand, such an opportunity might not come the boy's way again.

"Well, I won't stand in your way," his father told him at last. "Go, if you're a mind to."

"I'm a goin'!" Caleb sang out eagerly when he and Ira returned from the vessel later. "The master says if I do my work well I'm to be paid in silver same's the rest when the cargo's unloaded."

His face was glowing, and he seemed to have grown inches taller as he stood before them with his announcement. Already it was as if he were removed from Marguerite and the round-eyed half-sisters and brother who would stay behind.

"He'll be grown up when he comes back," she thought with a queer twinge of envy, " 'most a man."

It was strange in the log house and clearing when Ira and Caleb had sailed away on the *Fortunate Star*. It seemed especially quiet and empty after all the bustle of their last preparations. Dolly and Marguerite had mended their few patched articles of clothing, and Caleb had amazed Marguerite by entrusting to her care his drying squirrel skins and the little vessel he had carved from wood that winter.

"You watch out for 'em for me, Maggie," he had said, "an' I'll fetch you a token from Boston."

They had been gone a week, and now it was Marguerite who went each morning to Ira's post by the door to scratch another day lest they lose count. It pleased her to do this, to carry on Ira's custom, so that he should find it all in good order when he returned.

"Soon it will be the first of May," she told the children. "In Le Havre and all over France there will be dancing and merrymaking."

"What for will there be such doin's?" the twins questioned her as she sat with them on the doorstep.

"In honor of the spring," she explained, "and in England also, I have heard."

"Yes," Dolly joined in with unexpected volubility from indoors. "Many's the time I've heard my folks tell of it. They were out o' Somerset where there was a Maypole an' dancin' an' a Jack o' the Green every year "

"We had Maypoles too," Marguerite went on in eager reminiscence. "Oncle Pierre would play, and I have myself danced with the others and helped to braid the colored ribbons."

The children could not hear enough of this. They pressed Marguerite and their mother for more details, hanging on their every word.

"Couldn't we have one here?" Becky asked. "There's that pole out on the point, and Maggie would show us how to dance round it."

But such an idea was not encouraged. "Mercy, whoever heard o' such a thing?" Dolly exclaimed. "Haven't we got plenty to do plantin' an' findin' enough food to fill our stomachs every day without you must raise a Maypole too?"

"Besides," added Marguerite, "there must be bright streamers to weave about it, and we have none."

"Maybe Aunt Hepsa would give us some," urged Susan. "She's got lots o' colored cloth in her weavin' shed."

"You'd best not let your father hear such talk," warned their mother. "It's time you were all helpin' him, not gab-bin' away on the doorstep."

Even Marguerite and the children had been pressed into the work of planting. The plowing was only half-done when Ira had left, so Joel must continue this heavy work and the stump-pulling alone. Sometimes the twins were set to work with a homemade wooden rake and hoe, get-ting out stones, sticks, and snags of root from the earth. These tools were clumsy and too large for the children's hands, so Marguerite often helped when she was not fol-lowing Joel along the furrows he turned with such pains. They had a little corn left for seeding, and Seth had given them some barley and a few potatoes to be cut and planted. Joel showed the girl how to drop the corn and seeds in carefully, counting each one as if it were a nugget of gold. Up and down she went at his bidding, her bare feet tread-ing the damp, chill soil. There was to be another planting when the *Fortunate Star* brought Ira and Caleb and the new supplies, but meantime they must raise an early crop if all the mouths were to be fed before cold set in. Some-times at the end of these days the girl ached from head to foot with all the tramping and bending. She was slight and wiry, but this was work for a man or a half-grown boy.

Still it was beautiful out there in the strong spring sun-shine. Marguerite marveled at the swiftness with which the seasons changed in this northerly place. At home in France spring had come after a more leisurely fashion, but here, almost overnight it seemed, the earth turned from bleakness to vehement green. One day patches of snow and brown earth, and the next wild flowers under foot, and bushes of blossoming shadblow white in the woods. Already there were little new leaves on the appletree grafts and bayberry filling the air with spiciness from its fresh and springing green. Soon, Marguerite knew, there would be blue flags in the swampy land and then daisies to remind her of her true name.

"Everything makes haste in this place," she told herself as she went about her work. "I do believe that even the birds sing more and the flowers put on brighter colors because the season is so brief."

Whether this was true or not, Joel meant that it should be so on his part. Dolly rebuked him sometimes for working so hard and late. She could not get him to leave his patch of cleared land while there was so much as a ray of light to see by. He plowed and dug and chopped with a kind of fierce tirelessness. It was as if he had ceased to feel anything but the need to pour all his strength into the task before him. A curious light was in his eyes, which had sunk more deeply into their hollows after the hardships of the winter months. His back stayed stooped when he returned to the log house at night as if he had forgotten how to straighten it. Sometimes Marguerite heard Dolly remonstrating with him, begging him to pause a moment for rest or to take the snack of food she carried out to him.

"You can't go on this way, Joe," she would say. "No man can do the work o' three without killin' himself."

But he would only shake his head grimly as he stood

gulping the food and water she brought, his knotty brown hands so numb with gripping ax and crowbar that he could scarcely bend them to take what she held out.

"I've got to raise a good crop," he would answer, pushing the damp hair off his forehead. "Everything depends on that an' clearin' more land."

"I guess things can't never again be so bad as this year," she tried to encourage him. "Don't see how they could be if the Injuns just hold off."

Instinctively Dolly lowered her voice as she spoke. They all did now if they used the name. There had been quiet for so many months, but it was after just such a spell of peace that an attack might follow without so much as a sign of warning. Marguerite knew this, and that the dread of a raid was on them each night as they lay down to sleep. There had been less chance of it during the months of ice and cold, but with river and wood ways open, all the old fears were renewed. Besides, as she well remembered, on that first meeting Seth Jordan had spoken of spring as a bad time. That was when they had come before and burned down Flint's house. What would they say, she wondered, if they could know of her strange meeting with an Indian on Christmas Eve?

She often went out in the skiff with the children to catch fresh fish. There were plenty near shore in the channel waters, and even Patty and Jacob were now skillful at baiting their hooks and bringing up cod and haddock. They caught flounder, too, and silvery pollock, and by using a net and stick of Caleb's inventing they could often pull up lobsters and crabs. At low tide they often went to the little inlet on the other side of their eastern point, where they could dig clams for Dolly to cook into chowder or bake in seaweed to be eaten out of their shells.

"That's how the Injun's do it," Susan remarked the first time they tried this method. "Aunt Hepsa, she says there's old heaps over on Sunday Island where they used to come."

"Well, just so long's they keep away from here, I don't care how or where they eat their clams," said her mother from the fire.

The fresh food gave them all better appetites, as did the work in the sea air. By early May the children all began to look sturdier again and to have their old color and freckles. Dolly got out all her pieces and began contriving how to make them larger dresses and how to lengthen Marguerite's old holland. But turn and twist as best she could, there was no making extra yards to keep pace with their growing bodies.

"I declare if you young ones keep on this way," she sighed one night, "I'll be put to making *one* decent dress, an' the rest of you can stay indoors whilst one's wearin' it."

But before that happened, there were new cares to fill her mind, for Joel stumbled on a rooty snag just as he sprang away from a tree he was felling. Thrown to his knees, he was not able to clear the trunk as it crashed down, pinning him fast by one leg. He was not within hailing distance of the house, and so it was only Pumpkin's barking that brought the others to him. At first the children paid no heed to the dog's leaps and whimperings, but finally his tugs at Dolly's apron and his short starts towards the woods made them suspicious. They found Joel unconscious, and it was only by their combined tuggings that they were able to free his leg from the fallen tree.

Dolly and Marguerite scarcely spoke while they worked. They made no replies to the children's frightened questions, and it was only when they heard him begin to groan that they dared pause to wipe his face of its sweat and dirt. He was a heavy man for all his gauntness, and it seemed to the girl that they would never get him back to the house though it was hardly a quarter of a mile distant. They had to crawl along, Marguerite supporting his injured leg and moving backwards, while Dolly grasped him firmly under the armpits and guided them over the rough places.

The children she sent on to make the bed ready and set the kettle to heat. It was almost dark when they got him under the covers. Marguerite volunteered to row over and fetch Hepsa Jordan at once, but Dolly would not hear of it at such an hour and with no man to help her. So between them they did what they could to ease Joel of his pain. He was conscious now, for the moving had roused him with every jolt. They bathed a great bruise on one side of his head under his lank, matted hair, and washed away the blood and dirt from his leg. It was badly crushed and evidently broken in more than one spot for already the bone rose in several ugly lumps.

"If we don't get that in splints tonight those bones'll likely come through the flesh," said Dolly, practical even in her despair. "You go fetch me two flat pieces o' wood, Maggie, as smooth an' thin as you can find, while I lay this witchhazel water on."

Down in the cove Marguerite remembered to have seen pieces of wood worn smooth and thin from sea and sun. She sped over the path and stones and from one driftwood pile to another, seeking the finest of these. At last she had two of a proper size and smoothness and back she hurried to help Dolly bind them on over the wrappings of wet linen. Dolly had sacrificed one of her treasured dowry sheets for this, there being nothing left to use since Debby's burns. Joel was talking now, a faint, feverish jargon that caused the children to peer at him with more than their usual awe.

"He's out o' his head with the pain," said Dolly as they lashed the homemade splints tight with leather thongs. "There, Joe, don't take on so," she added, taking his hand between hers, "we won't touch it no more."

Marguerite left them together while she went to prepare the supper. The children must eat, and there was herb tea to be brewed from a dried bunch Aunt Hepsa had given them. Perhaps, she thought, this would ease him enough to make him sleep.

Ever since Debby's accident there had been an agreement that a white sheet hung out from the old pole on the point would be a sign to the Jordans on Sunday Island that help was needed. Already it was too dark for this, and next morning when Marguerite woke she saw with dismay that fog had come in from open sea blotting out even the nearer ledges. Sunday Island might have been a hundred miles distant with this chill gray wall between them.

"If only Caleb were here," she thought as she rose to peer out at the damp and dripping trees beyond the window panes; "or that I had learned to use the compass!"

It was not enough that she could pull the oars sturdily. She and Dolly both knew the dangers of setting out in a fog with only one's feelings for guide. People could row in circles for hours on end; and worse than that, they might head straight for open sea and come to grief on dangerous reefs.

"There's nothin' for it but to tend him the best way we can till it clears," Dolly Sargent told her. "He's 'most crazy with the pain, but we've got to keep that splint on firm if the bone's to knit."

Marguerite could hear Joel groaning and moving restlessly on the bed in the next room while she made the children's breakfast and tried to keep them from being too noisy. When she carried a bowl of hasty pudding in to him it seemed unbelievable to see him lying there so weak and feverish, laid low as completely as one of the great spruces his ax had so often felled. His eyes were bright in their dark sockets, his lips parched, and he called for water continually.

"What's the day?" he asked her querulously as she was slipping away from his bedside.

"It is the ninth of May," she told him. "I have but just been out to scratch another mark on the post."

"The ninth o' May," he murmured faintly; "so late, and so much still to be done. Here I lie, an' Ira an' Caleb can't be back for a fortnight at best."

He turned his face away with another low groan, and Marguerite, being unable to think of any remark to give him comfort, went back to the fire and the children. She had her hands full between them and the fire and cooking, for Dolly must stay by Joel's bed to keep him quiet and put fresh compresses of witchhazel water on the swellings around the splints. Marguerite and the children fetched wood and water and fished or dug clams at low tide by turns. Never had a day seemed so long, or a fog so heavy and determined.

"Ain't it goin' to clear, Maggie?" Jacob asked a dozen times before it turned dark.

"It can't till this east wind shifts," Susan would answer. "You'd ought to know that by this time."

"The gulls know it," Marguerite pointed out. "See how they sit facing the east so that their feathers shall not be blown the wrong way. It was even so in Le Havre along the quay when the fog was in. But," she found herself giving a discouraged sigh, "I do not think there were ever such fogs as these."

In spite of all that Dolly could do, Joel Sargent's fever increased as the day wore on. Toward evening he began to wander in his mind and to talk in half-delirious fragments that were frightening to hear. Sometimes he shouted orders to Ira and Caleb about the chopping and plowing, and sometimes he started up in bed, reaching for his musket and insisting that he heard Indians about. Pumpkin lay by the bedroom door, his head raised in a plaintive, puzzled way, uttering low whimperings when the sick man grew especially excited.

"He knows Pa's hurt bad," Jacob pointed out. "If he could swim as far as he can run I guess he'd go after Aunt Hepsa."

"I doubt she could do more for him than we're doin'," his mother said wearily. "But she's got more witchhazel, an' ours is runnin' low."

"We could get you more of the bark to steep," Marguerite told her. "It will not be flowing now—still, we could cut it roots and all. I could find that place again."

Dolly Sargent looked dubious. "I daren't let you an' the young ones go so far alone in the woods," she said. "Much as he needs it, I'd be fearful every moment you were gone."

That night Marguerite prayed that the fog might lift. She prayed fervently, with all the phrases she could remember and with many added ones of her own making. But still the wind stayed east and still the thick gray wall of blowing damp pressed up from the water. Joel slept in fitful snatches, with Dolly getting what rest she could as she sat the nights through beside him. She looked nearly as worn as he, and her voice was sharp with anxiety when she spoke to the children. It was two days and two nights since the accident. There was nothing left now with which to dress the injured leg except cold water from the spring. Joel Sargent seemed quieter, but this was from weakness, and he still had spells of wanderings in his mind.

"I've heard Aunt Hepsa say there was healing in that brown kelp down on the beach," Marguerite suggested on the third morning, when the fog still held. "There's a lot of it down in the farther cove. Let the children go with me and bring some."

"Well, go along then," Dolly had consented half-heartedly. "It would be coolin' and no harm to try."

Taking the old splint basket, the five set off together with Pumpkin. It was still some hours till noon, and the sun was making valiant attempts to burn off the fog. Their spirits rose somewhat at this and at being away from the house and the sound of Joel's moans and hard breathing. One of the remaining hens had laid an egg, which was entrusted to Susan's care.

"That ought to make him better," said Becky. "An egg is 'most as good a cure as herbs, I guess."

"I had an egg all by myself when I cut my head open," put in Jacob reminiscently, "an' it made me well."

They moved on more cheerfully after this. Marguerite carried the basket and walked ahead with Patty at her side. They went through a patch of spruce woods near shore because it was easier walking than along the beach. Pumpkin bounded forward, his nose to the ground and his tail alert. Suddenly they saw him stop and sniff, head raised and tail stiffened warningly. A low growl came next, and a shiver passed under the yellow fur along his back. Instantly Marguerite laid her finger to her lips and caught the two younger ones' hands.

"Quiet," she whispered, "there may be danger."

A year before they might have run or cried out, but they had learned better now. With the wariness of the woods they drew together in silence. They were almost within sight of the cove. The dog's head was turned questioningly in that direction even before there came a sound of pebbles striking one against another. Marguerite felt her throat tighten. A chill ran along her spine as she listened with the children's warm bodies pressing close.

"Injuns," she heard Jacob whisper, and she knew that the same dread was on them all.

"Stay here," she whispered back, "and keep fast hold of Pumpkin, while I go to look."

They stared at her aghast, but she found herself slipping from their clinging hands. Dropping on her knees she began to wriggle towards the bluff above the cove. She knew the scraggling trees at the edge would shield her from sight, and she made for a gap between the spruces. Sharp twigs and roots tore at her hair and face, scratching her bare arms and legs as she crept along by inches.

"Quiet. Quiet. Quiet," something seemed to be saying over and over within her, but perhaps it was only the beating of her own heart as she went.

And now another sound came to her from the woods— a long-drawn call, birdlike, yet human. She shivered to hear it, but still she crept on. Twice the call came, and twice it was answered from the cove below. She was close enough now to peer over the edge. It seemed, in that moment of time that she crouched there, as if the cove were alive with moving brown bodies. Several canoes were beached and others gliding in. She caught the flash of dipping paddles and the brightness of blankets. After that she waited for nothing but sped back to the children.

They were standing where she had left them in a scared little group with Pumpkin held firmly in their midst. His eyes rolled uneasily though he did not bark. It was as if he sensed the nearness of old enemies, whining in soft distrust.

"Watch every step," warned Marguerite. "Do not let a twig snap."

Without a word they followed her, taking care to set their bare feet on the moss, avoiding roots and fallen branches. Susan stumbled, breaking the precious egg, but still they hurried on. Once again the queer call was thrown out on the air behind them. It seemed they would never reach the log house, but at last they came out of the woods into the clearing. The sight of the brown logs, the broad doorstep, and the smoke at the chimney gave Marguerite a sense of security, for a moment only.

Dolly met them at the door with her finger to her lips.

"He's just got to sleep in there," she told them. "Take care not to wake him—"

Then her face grew pale as she saw their faces and guessed the truth.

"Injuns—in the cove!" they gasped. "They didn't see us, not yet!"

Without a word she dragged them all into the house and barred the door and the inside shutters. Then they drew together, taking counsel in frightened whispers.

"Shall we get down the musket?" asked Susan.

"What's the good?" answered her mother. "There's not more 'n a charge or two o' powder left, an' I'm a poor hand at firin'. How many of 'em did you reckon there was, Maggie?"

"I do not know," she told her, "but many in the cove where we go for clams. They were building a fire, and there are more in the woods because they answered the call.

As she spoke a thought flashed into her mind. It was almost as if she had not thought at all; as if the words she heard herself saying were unknown to her.

"Maybe they have not come to harm us," she said. "Maybe if I went down to them with food they would not scalp us or burn the house."

Dolly protested and the children clung to her crying, but she kept repeating the idea over and over. Now that it had come she grew more sure of herself. She put aside the children's hands and moved over to the cupboard. First she lifted out the remaining bag of parched corn, and then as she took up the keg of maple syrup she felt Dolly's hand on her shoulder.

"Have you lost your wits?" she heard her saying.

She shook her head and wiggled away. A queer sense of power possessed her, even when Dolly caught her once more by the shoulders and began to shake her fiercely.

"You put those things down!" she ordered. "Do you hear what I say?"

Marguerite shook herself free of the older woman. She stood facing her with the remnants of their food at her feet and a grim determination about her lips.

"I am going down there," she said steadily. "If they have come to kill us they will take the things anyway." The clearness with which she spoke amazed her as much as the others.

The children stared at her dully, and even Dolly stood still and unprotesting. Joel groaned from the next room, and she returned to his side.

Marguerite caught up the corn and ran to unbolt the door. "Children," she said with her hand on the latch, "you do what I tell you, no matter what."

"Yes, Maggie," they piped faintly.

She signaled them to tie Pumpkin fast inside and then to help her set the food on the doorstep. In silence they did her bidding, their eyes large with terrified curiosity.

The sun, which had for so long been trying to burn away the fog, had at last succeeded in breaking through. Already the mists were dividing, with blue water and sky showing in ever-widening gaps. The pointed tops of the highest trees on Sunday Island rose sharply out of the blowing gray. An hour ago they would have hailed this so joyfully, but now there was no time for rejoicing. Even then a dark figure was moving from tree to tree.

With the fleetness of a shadow it came on toward them,

and then all the trees seemed alive with other lean, swift figures. From the house Pumpkin let forth a long, deep wail, and the children shrank together by the doorstep.

"Allons," Marguerite told herself, "one must appear brave."

After that she was aware only of brown hands into which she doled the corn. She dared not look at the faces above them. She must only watch the kernels, to make them fill all the hands held out to her. But the bag was empty and still they reached out. The hands were plucking at her skirt, insistent and terrifying.

She wrenched herself free and reached for the syrup bucket and wooden spoon. Dipping this in she brought it up sticky and golden, holding it out with a gesture that brought them clustering like bees round a hive. There would not be enough for all. Of that she was certain as she stood aside watching them jostle and snatch for a taste of the sweet. It did not seem as if they could be real, and yet she knew they must be. There were some eight or ten of them, all tall, strong men, and doubtless more in the cove and woods. She steadied herself against the doorframe while she tried to think what to do next.

"What'll we do when it's gone, Maggie?" the twins whispered, pressing close.

She looked across to the Channel and Sunday Island, now clear of the fogbank. The Jordan house was plain once more in its green field, and her mind called up a momentary picture of Aunt Hepsa moving in safety about her kitchen or the weaving shed. Only if they saw the log house in flames would the Jordans know what had befallen their neighbors, and then it would be too late. As her eyes traveled sea and shore for some sign of help they lighted on the old pole on the point that Joel and Ira had used for hoisting heavier goods from the beach when they first landed. She remembered how the children had teased their mother to make a Maypole there.

"A Maypole," she said aloud, and the next moment she was making for the house and Dolly Sargent's pine chest.

The group about the syrup bucket was still busy licking and scraping. But she heard an ugly murmur as she passed. She could not tell what it meant, though she guessed that there was disagreement among them. She caught the flash of a hunting knife stuck in a leather belt and a hatchet in another. If these once came out and there was bloodshed—she shivered and hurried on.

Dolly stood with the children at the door, ready to bar it at the first sign of attack. Marguerite pressed by them without a word and threw up the lid of the chest. The one remaining dower sheet of white linen lay there along with her length of red cloth from Abby Welles. She seized both and a knife and began hacking and tearing the cloth into long strips. Dolly cried out in dismay and started to go to her. But she dared not leave her place by the door. The linen was so firm and finely woven Marguerite had hard work to tear it to pieces. She clawed in frantic desperation till it yielded to her hands with a ripping noise. After that she waited for nothing but to catch up a hammer and some nails.

"Come," she said to the children, "we will have our Maypole now."

Already she was out of the door and beckoning to them with the torn strips of linen about her. Dolly called sharply to her to come back, and the children continued to peer at her fearfully, hanging back beside their mother.

"Quick!" she commanded them, summoning all her power into her voice as she had forced it into her hands when the cloth had resisted her. "You must come!"

She had no thought beyond time and those brown bodies in the dooryard, yet she found herself working with a strange sureness and speed. The pole had been a tree cut from the nearby woods and was thick and sturdy. Where its branches had been lopped, rough crotches gave her footing. By holding the nails between her teeth and keeping the cloth around her shoulders she was able to climb up. It was not far in actual feet, but no ladder had ever seemed higher. At last her fingers touched the top. She braced her bare feet more firmly in the crotches and called to Susan to climb up after her. Between them they managed to pound the nails into the wood and cloth. The linen strips fluttered limply in the spring breeze, some thin and frayed, others stouter and jaggedly torn, with the one red streamer, knotted in two places to make it long enough, showing like a scarlet thread. Even as she stood there below it Marguerite knew with a queer sense of wonder that there had never been such a Maypole raised before—not in the Old World nor the New.

It was the last thought of which she was conscious. After that her mind was a confused jumble of pictures in which she saw herself moving as clearly as she saw the rest—the Indians and the children. She remembered the curiously peering black eyes under upstanding crests of hair; and the brightness of knife blades and hatchets all about her. She heard Patty cry out in terror at the touch

of brown fingers, and she heard her own voice telling the child to be still.

"Dance!" she cried to them sharply. "This way!"

She caught at a streamer and began to go through the motions for them, moving it now under, now over, those beside her. One of the Indians grunted and tried to do likewise. The men's hands were tugging at the strips of cloth now, and the children were hopping up and down between the brown bodies. It was not easy to hold the strands. Over and over again Marguerite must untangle these and show them how to weave the cloth over one another's. Jacob and Patty were as awkward as the Indians, who moved round the pole holding fast to their ends of linen with expressions of curious wonder. They were like a lot of grown children pleased with a new game. When one tired, another would take his place, since there were more Indians than pieces of cloth. How the nails held was a marvel to Marguerite. By this time she had given up all idea of braiding the strands round the pole. All that mattered now was that they should continue about it from moment to moment.

"We cannot stop," she gasped to the children as she passed them in the dance. "Faster—see!"

Her own breath came very short, and she could no longer feel her feet moving under her. Her hair tumbled about her shoulders, and she felt Grand'mère's ring on its cord thumping, thumping under her cotton dress. Drops of sweat rose on her forehead. They ran down her face and into her eyes till she could not tell the children from the Indians moving about her. The sun on the water and the streamers made a dizzy blur.

"I must go on, I must not stop," she kept telling herself, though now she hardly remembered the reason why.

And then there was a sound of ripping cloth and splintering wood, and she knew that the Maypole was toppling. The children's voices were calling to her through a great buzzing and roaring in her head. She rubbed the wet out of her eyes and tried to go to them, but the Indians were in the way. They were struggling over the wreck of the Maypole. Knives flashed and there were shrill cries as they fought each other to get a piece of the cloth. Marguerite knew there was no time to lose, and she called to the children to follow her.

She felt herself running with them towards the log house, when a tall brown figure rose up in her path. It was too late to turn back or hide. There was not even time enough to cry out a warning to the children. They crouched at her skirts. She could feel their hot, panting breath behind her, and she knew that they were all waiting for the blow to fall. Why was it so long in falling, she wondered?

"*Noël*," she heard a voice above her say quite clearly, and she looked up into a lean, coppery face with a ragged scar running along one cheek.

Slowly the chill left her, and it no longer hurt to draw her breath.

"Do not fear him," she told the children. "He is a friend."

Even as she spoke she saw him point to Oncle Pierre's gilt button, which he wore proudly among the fringes of his leather coat. He smiled at her and motioned toward the house, making her understand that they were to go back. Already he was moving off to join the others, and still Marguerite had no breath left to say even a single "merci."

Telling their mother of it later in the log house, the twins insisted that Maggie and the strange Indian had talked together in French, but she had no recollection of any but his one word of greeting. Indeed she remembered far less than the children, who told how the other Indians had followed the scar-faced one off into the woods.

"An' they all had bits o' the sheet," Susan explained. "They must have tore it up into little pieces."

Marguerite listened to them dully from the corner where she had flung herself beside Pumpkin. The dog was licking her face, and she knew Dolly hovered between the two rooms, now going to Joel, who had hurt himself badly tearing off his bandages to try and get his musket when he heard the Indians, and now returning to make sure the children were safe again. She heard Dolly speak to her as well as the others, but their words went past her like falling rain. She was too spent to lay hold of their meaning. There seemed to be no feeling left in her—none at all.

She did not even rouse herself when she heard the twins report that the Jordans' dory was coming over from Sunday Island; and when Seth and Ethan appeared at the door she still did not stir from the floor. They had come because they had seen a flutter of white from the point. They had not been able to make it out, but they had guessed that something queer was going on. Their faces were grave as they went in to look at Joel's crushed leg and listen to Dolly and the children.

"You mean to tell me she went out there an' passed food

to those Injuns an' then rigged that Maypole an' got 'em dancin' round it?" Seth Jordan's voice came breaking through the haze that had settled over Marguerite.

"Yes, she done it," she heard Dolly's voice making reply. "She saved us, all by herself."

"It's a miracle—sure," Seth was saying. "I guess there ain't many girls would be so brave."

Marguerite shook off the heaviness long enough to answer them.

"I did not feel brave," she admitted from her corner.

She could not say more than this for some days to come, not indeed till Joel's leg was beginning to mend and they were all breathing more easily again. Aunt Hepsa and one of the men came over each day with food and soothing herbs to quiet the sick man's pain, and it was to them and Dolly that she finally confided the story of her Christmas Eve meeting with the Indian. She confessed this timidly, though no one raised a word of blame against her. Their praise was very sweet, even if she still continued to feel that they must be talking of another girl when they spoke proudly of what she had done.

"What beats me," Aunt Hepsa asked her more than once, "is how you come to think o' such a thing as that Maypole?"

But Marguerite could not tell her. She did not know herself.

"It just came into my mind," she could only answer lamely.

She did not tell them that she mourned the loss of her red cloth. She could not help remembering how smooth and rich it had been, and how she planned to cut and sew it. But perhaps Hepsa Jordan guessed this, for one day she brought over the half-made patchwork quilt and put all the pieces into Marguerite's lap.

"There," she said in answer to the girl's questioning look, "I want you should have it for your own."

"But—but not the 'Delectable Mountains'?" Marguerite touched the jagged blues and buffs with an awed forefinger.

"It's yours, to finish an' keep," the old woman insisted. "You always did fancy that pattern right from the first, an' I don't know who's earned a better right to it. There, now, don't you say a word," she added at the girl's bewildered thanks. "When it's all pieced I'll help you quilt it, an' then you'll have one thing ready against the time you marry."

Dolly and the children came out on the doorstep to see and admire the deep blue patches fitting so neatly into the buff ones. Marguerite's hands trembled with eagerness to take the first stitches in it.

"I should like to make a ballad about it," she said as she bent over the squares, "like 'Calico Bush.'"

"Maybe you will, child," Aunt Hepsa nodded, "an' maybe you'll be in one yourself someday. I wouldn't wonder but what after we're all dead an' gone folks'll sail by here an' look over to that point an' ask how it come to be called 'The Maypole.' Yes," she told them, "Seth's written it in so on his chart, an' I guess that's how it'll be called."

They sat for a long time in the sun, busy with work and talk. Nearby the children moved about. They were making a little garden in the yard, setting out some slips from Sunday Island under the old woman's direction. Now and again Dolly Sargent came from the sick man's room to stand a moment in the doorway.

"Joel's frettin' over his crops again," she said. "He's fearful Ira won't get back in time to tend 'em, but I tell him long's I can see the young ones all safe an' in sight—"

She broke off as her eyes went past the busy children to Debby's little mound at the edge of the clearing. Marguerite and Hepsa Jordan followed her look and knew what she must be thinking.

"What the earth covers we must forget," the old woman told her, her words fitting themselves to the click of her knitting needles in such a way that they went deep into the girl's mind, till she found herself inwardly repeating them—"What the earth covers we must forget."

"Yes, I guess that's how it has to be," sighed Dolly, and she moved heavily back into the house.

It was almost June again when the *Fortunate Star* hove in sight, her sails square and shining as she made for the Channel between the outer islands. Marguerite was at work in the cornfield when Jacob ran to her with the news, and she set down the hoe and sped with him to join the rest. They gathered on the point in an eager little group, from which one or another would break away to bring news of the ship's progress to Joel Sargent, who still lay bound to his bed.

"How long since she sailed away, Maggie?" the children kept asking her.

"Five weeks an' three days tomorrow," she told them when she had counted over the marks on the doorpost.

Now she was heading in, keeping to the seaward side of Sunday Island the better to clear the ledges. They could see her topsails like square-cut clouds, moving behind the tallest trees, and it seemed she would never come to anchor off their eastern point.

"I declare it lifts the heart right up in me to see her," said Dolly. "Seems like I couldn't 'a' waited another day."

None of them thought of food, though it was long past noon before the boats were lowered and the men rowed in.

"There they are," shouted Jacob, "I can see Uncle Ira an' Caleb in the first boat!"

A queer shyness overcame Marguerite as she watched them land. She hung back from the rest, conscious of her old dress and bare feet. It was different now that they had been to such far ports as Portsmouth, Salem and Boston. Besides, she could see that Caleb was inches taller than he had been. He wore a man's coat, and his breeches were tucked into rough boots such as the others had. He carried himself like a man, too, and swung a heavy pack easily across his shoulders.

"Hey, Maggie," he called out as he spied her, and his voice was deep for all that his hair and freckles were unchanged.

They talked so late that night that Jacob and Patty fell fast asleep with their hands clutching the wooden top and jumping jack one of the sailors had made for them. There were presents for everyone—cloth and needles for Dolly; a china mug for each of the twins, and for Marguerite a box with a bird painted on the lid.

"I was all for gettin' Maggie some yarn or calico," Ira explained when it was brought out, "but Caleb was sure she'd fancy this better."

Caleb flushed darkly at this reference.

"Looked like 'twas some kind of a foreign popinjay," was all he would say, but he took pains to show her that a glass bead had been cunningly set in the wood to represent the bird's eye.

"It is beautiful," she told him, "and I shall take care to keep it indoors where the real birds will not grow jealous of its more handsome feathers."

She could not bear to put it away for the night or to shut out the sight of the well-stocked shelves and cupboard. It had been a good voyage, and Ira was sure that when he had the crops harvested in the fall, the Captain would take him on another, which would mean he could start saving toward the house he planned to build for Abby on his land. He was bringing her a coral pin, which Dolly considered a shameless piece of extravagance. Long after Marguerite and the children were under their covers she heard the voices talking on and on around Joel's bed, and she guessed from fragments that came to her through the open door that Dolly was enlarging on what the children had told of the Indian raid. She fell asleep at last, but not till she had heard Ira and Caleb climb to their old place in the loft overhead. It comforted her to hear the wood creak under their feet once more.

The *Fortunate Star* was to stay off their point for another day while the crew rested and carried fresh water aboard. The children were up at sunrise in their eagerness to make sure it was still there. Marguerite slipped out with them in the early light. The water was a quiet stretch of silver on which the vessel loomed dark and ghostly, with all its canvas reefed and each line and mast black against the brightness. It seemed strange to see it there, resting so easily and at home off their point, and to know that before another night no trace would be left to show that it had ever been there.

Once more there was plenty of meal and molasses for breakfast and fresh fish that Caleb had been out early to catch. Soon afterward the Channel began to be dotted with boats, for besides those on Sunday Island neighbors to the east and southwest had seen the vessel while she was still far out at sea and had rowed over to visit her. Timothy Welles had brought Abby along in his sloop; the Stanleys were all packed tight into their old dory, and Seth and Ethan Jordan were aboard the *Fortunate Star* early, bargaining with the master and mate for fresh supplies of food and such merchandise as she carried from Boston. Ira and Caleb had promised to take the children aboard, and Marguerite would have gone with them but that Joel Sargent called to her from his bed.

"I want a word with you, Maggie," he said, and the seriousness of his manner filled her with alarm as she went in to stand before him.

Joel Sargent was not given to many words, least of all to her, and she had been too busy looking after the children and working about the house to exchange many with him since his accident. He was beginning to look more like himself, she thought, as he lay there under the Rising Sun quilt, but his face was still gaunt and his eyes deeply sunken. It seemed strange to the girl to see his great, knotted hands stretched idle on the covers instead of grasping ax or plow.

"How old have you got to be now, Maggie?" he asked her.

"Thirteen," she told him, "I will be fourteen by next November."

"Yes," he said, "I took you at twelve an' you're bound-out to me for six years till you're eighteen. You recollect how 'twas agreed back in Marblehead?"

She nodded wonderingly, and waited for him to continue.

"You've been a good girl, Maggie," he told her, "an' a brave one. I ain't said much, but I know grit when I see it, an' you've got more'n your share." She flushed with pleasure, and after a slight pause he went on. "I've talked it over with Dolly an' Ira. We want to do the right thing by you, an' it seems only fair to let you go to your folks when the chance comes."

"But I have none," Marguerite replied. "They are dead."

"I know," he explained. "'Twas your own people I meant. You see, it's this way. The *Fortunate Star* is headin' for the Saint Lawrence an' Quebec. There's fightin' up that way between us an' the French an' Indians, but they'll let her through because she's fetchin' supplies. Now the master'll take you along too."

"To Quebec?"

"Yes. It's in French hands, an' there's a convent where they'd look out for you. I guess likely they'd ship you back to France if you wanted. Anyhow, you'd be with your own kind again."

"You mean that you are freeing me from those papers they drew up when you took me to work for you?"

"Yes, you've earned your freedom. I'll have the mate write it out so there'll be no mistakin' that. She sails with the tide, so you've got an hour or so to make yourself ready."

"Oh, but you are good! You are kind!" Impulsively Marguerite caught up his hand from the bed and pressed it to her lips with a half-forgotten French gesture. "I will not forget it, but—but I must think first."

"Very well," he told her, "only don't take too long about it, an' remember it's a chance that ain't likely to come again."

Her head was buzzing like a hive of bees as she went out of the house. It had all come about so quickly, and now she must make up her mind before the tide reached the line of brown kelp and driftwood along the pebble beach. Already the water was halfway there, and the outermost rocks of Old Horse Ledges were covered. As she stepped over the doorsill Pumpkin rose and pressed close to her, his muzzle laid to her hand, his nose moist against her fingers. Some sticks and bits of burr were caught in his fur, and she bent to pick them out.

"Poor fellow," she said, "you were glad of your good breakfast, eh?"

He followed her over to the point, and they sat down together on the ground where bunchberry blossoms were beginning to show star-shaped white petals. By late July these would have turned to bright scarlet berries. The children would gather them and make wreaths and chains to wear as she had taught them, but she would not be there to see. It gave her a queer pang to think of this, and of their crops, and of the first apples on the little trees being gathered without her. Beside her, half-buried in leaves and flowers, the old Maypole lay as it had fallen the day the Indians had come. She could still see it with the fluttering strips of cloth. She could still feel the beating of her own heart as she forced herself to dance around it with the children.

Feeling inside her dress for Grand'mère's gold ring, she drew it out and held it tightly between her two hands as if the touch of it must help her. Grand'mère would like her to go back to France; to be among French people once more. Of that she felt certain. She knew it would pain her to hear her granddaughter answer to a name like Maggie. Even more would it pain her to know that Marguerite had not set foot inside a church for more than a twelvemonth, and that it was as long again since her fingers had told rosary beads.

"One cannot remember when there is so much to be done," she found herself saying as if in answer.

But if she returned to the Convent it would all come back to her—her prayers and her devotions, along with her skill with needle and thread. Joel Sargent had spoken of a convent in Quebec. Now that she thought of it she remembered to have heard mention of such a one by the Sisters in Le Havre. The most pious Mother Superior and Sisters had been sent to establish the faith in New France. They had carried their precious relics and bells across the sea with them. It was said that all was as devout and well ordered there as if the stones of the walls were not freshly hewn from the solid rock and under the shadow of wild forests at the edge of the wilderness. It would be good to be with the Sisters again; to move quietly, contentedly through the hours to the ringing of a chapel bell. Yes, she would like that, and yet—

The shouts of the children in the cove below broke into her thoughts. She sighed and turned her head away as if she would not let them batter so on the doors of her mind.

Over on Sunday Island a wisp of smoke rose from the Jordan chimney, and she knew Aunt Hepsa must be busy over her fire. She had only to shut her eyes to picture that pleasant kitchen and the old woman bending over her pots or loom or quilting frame. Even the Sisters in the convent in Le Havre were not so wise and kind as Aunt Hepsa. How could she go away, with the blue and buff quilt unfinished and all the summer's wool to be spun and woven? If she went now she would not see the laurel grow pink in the upper pasture, nor hear again the ballad of "Calico Bush."

The children were waving and calling to her from the water. Their shrill voices came clearly on the air as Ira and Caleb rowed them back to shore. Pumpkin rose and barked a response. She, too, rose involuntarily. They would be hungry, and most likely Caleb would have fish for her to cook. She turned to go back over the rough ground to the house, her bare feet knowing the hollow and rooty places so that she had no need to look down as she went.

They were hoisting the sales of the *Fortunate Star*. She could see some of the men climbing aloft and others on deck and rowing between it and the cove. Already it seemed straining against the anchor chains that held it fast. As she thought of it moving out of the Channel and herself on board, she felt suddenly chill and lonely. It was as if she had died and all the life of this place of which she had been part was going on without her.

"Maggie," the children were running up the steep bank to meet her, "Caleb says you're goin' away, but you wouldn't, would you?"

Jacob was the first to reach her, the scar on his forehead showing more white and jagged because his face was so red and breathless.

"You ain't goin' away on the vessel?" he panted, catching at her hand. "Say you ain't!"

"No," she heard herself telling him quietly, "I shall stay right here and cook your dinner."

It was late afternoon before the *Fortunate Star* got clear of the ledges and nearer islands. They watched her from the point till her sails were no more than a bright speck in the northeast.

"She's headin' round by those French hills you fancy so, Maggie," Ira pointed out. "Sure you ain't sorry you're not aboard her?"

Marguerite shook her head with a faint smile.

"Ma says you're foolish not to take the chance when you had it," Susan told her, pressing close, "but she's glad you didn't, an' I am too."

"So am I!" echoed Becky. "Ain't you glad, too, Caleb?"

"Well, maybe I am an' maybe I ain't!" he told them, wrinkling his face up in the impish grin Marguerite had once so dreaded. "But anyhow she's got more sense 'n the lot o' you put together!"

"Now it's out o' sight!" cried Jacob, running toward the house with the news.

Marguerite lingered on the point after the rest had gone. The air was spicy with salt and fresh bay leaves. Soon the sun would be going down behind the islands, but just in these few moments before it disappeared the line of Mount Desert hills stood out very deep and blue—almost as blue, she thought, as the "Delectable Mountains" on her quilt pattern.